Lawrence Conquest

Feeding Ambition

_____

A Novella in Four Courses

BLOOD BOUND BOOKS

ISBN 978-0-9849782-0-5

Artwork by Blacktop Brigade –
www.theblacktopbrigade.com

Printed in the United States of America

First Edition

Anthologies Available from Blood Bound Books:

Rock 'N' Roll is Dead: Dark Tales Inspired by Music

Night Terrors: An Anthology of Horror

Unspeakable: A New Breed of Terror

D.O.A.: Extreme Horror Collection

Seasons in the Abyss: Flash Fiction Anthology

Steamy Screams: Erotic Horror Anthology

Novels & Novellas:

Scarecrow & The Madness by Craig Saunders & Robert Essig

Monster Porn by KJ Moore

At The End of All Things by Stony Graves

The Sinner by K. Trap Jones

"He who is greedy is always in want."

-Horace

"The flesh endures the storms of the present alone: the mind, those of the past and future as well as the present. Gluttony is a lust of the mind."

-Thomas Hobbes

"Fame. I wanna live forever."

-Irene Cara

Mixed Seafood, Including Lobster And Calamari
(Serves Two)

The restaurant was a modern affair, all clean lines and open spaces. Slatted blinds along one wall held the local populace at bay, the shadows of their passing rendered indistinct and vague. The opposite wall was dominated by a succession of hanging plasma screens, their glowing surfaces rippling with artfully amorphous blue and green static. The effect made the screens appear to be windows onto another world, offering Oliver a tantalizing glimpse of a landscape partially obscured by driving rain. Forget the reality outside, the screens seemed to say, forget the crowds, the noise, the unrelieved stress of living in London. Forget the stares, the childish catcalls, the ever-present threat of violent death that comes with your given profession. At least for a while.

A glowing pastel tube extruded from the ceiling like some giant umbilical cord. The extravagant ceiling light cast a gentle ambience about the room, whilst flickering tealights lapped impotently at the remaining pools of gloom. A row of red leather couches divided the room in two. Facing alternately in opposite directions, their semi-circular backs described a looping series of 'S's across the wood paneled floor. The waiter led Oliver to one hip of this snakelike appendage, where a young woman sat ensconced like a semi-digested meal.

Rachel McFarland looked up at Oliver's approach and a smile instantly broke out across her gently freckled face. "Hello, Ollie. You found the place then?"

"Yes, fine, thanks." Oliver gave a token nod to the waiter, who was busy beating a backwards retreat. "I take it you've been here before, then?"

"Oh yes. It's something of a favorite of mine. The chef's a personal friend."

"Really?" Oliver smiled. "Don't tell me— you rescued him from a burning building?"

"Something like that. Fancy a drink?"

Oliver called out his order to the waiter, who had remained just within earshot whilst attempting to give the impression that he wasn't actually listening to the private conversation of his only two diners.

"Where is everybody anyway?" Oliver asked, gazing about him. Apart from himself, Rachel and the waiter, the only other inhabitant seemed to be a beer-bellied barman, who was busy pouring their drinks with professional nonchalance.

Rachel looked about the restaurant as if appreciating its emptiness for the first time. "Oh. I asked if we could have the place to ourselves tonight."

"No general public you mean? Not a bad idea. Where's the rest of the team, then?"

Rachel glanced shyly down at her menu. "Oh, Douggie doesn't get out much. And as for Lucy, well . . . It *is* getting rather late in the evening."

"So—it's just the two of us, then?"

Rachel looked up and offered a coy smile. "What's the matter, Oliver Rangarajan? You not keen on girls?"

Oliver blustered and busied himself with his menu, but his gaze kept creeping up to the woman

2

sat opposite him. He'd rarely seen Rachel out of her bulky armor, and he couldn't seem to stop stealing glances. Why hadn't he ever noticed how attractive she was before? In the soft candlelight, Rachel seemed almost incandescent, the paleness of her skin enhanced by the long scarlet tresses that washed about her head and shoulders in languid waves. The dress she wore was long and flowing, with a lace neckline that came up to her chin, and yet, it couldn't fully disguise the womanly curves beneath.

Oliver mentally chastised himself. He shouldn't be thinking like this. Rachel was a teammate. Worse than that, she was a friend.

All of a sudden, Oliver realized he had been staring, and worse, that Rachel had caught him doing so. "See something you like?"

He was frozen in the headlights of her gaze. Oliver opened his mouth to say something witty, but nothing emerged beyond an unintelligible wheeze.

"Anything you like *on the menu*?" Rachel sighed. "Honestly. Men. They can never make their minds up."

Feeling both relieved and disappointed to have been offered a lifeline, Oliver glanced back down at the meaningless piece of paper that he had supposedly been studying for the past five minutes. "Um. I don't know. It all looks so good. You're the regular—you decide."

Rachel shrugged non-committedly. "Well, why don't we start with an appetizer?"

"Sure. What are you having?"

Rachel laughed gently. "Oh, nothing for me, Ollie. A girl has to watch her figure. You know how it is."

Oliver glanced down wryly at his own corpulent frame and laughed. "I wish I did. With my powers I need all the saturated fats I can get." He paused for a moment, musing over the team's most recent experience. "Then again, I guess all that's about to change. Yeah, something a bit healthier for me, this time. Calamari looks good. You sure I can't tempt you?"

"It's OK, Ollie. Really." Rachel smiled. "Besides which, I've already eaten."

* * *

The Formica surface was all but obscured by plates, bowls and jars, each filled to the brim with various hot and cold foodstuffs. Pasta, meat, ice cream, pickled onions. Savory and sweet sat side by side in blissful contempt of culinary convention. Popcorn and chips. Curry and cornflakes. Indian, Chinese, and Mexican dishes mingled like delegates at a UN meeting. No carefully planned meal this, just a mindless, gargantuan buffet.

Seemingly seated motionless before her kitchen table, Rachel McFarland was in fact a blur of superhuman speed. Her limbs—quicker than any human eye could follow—made ghostly passes before her, giving her the appearance of a double amputee meditating before a cloud of smoke. Her head was angled back upon her shoulders, mouth open wide like a new-born chick at feeding time. A careful observer might have noticed the occasional bulge as something slid rapidly down Rachel's throat, or perhaps the sudden impact spatter of sauce darkening her blouse. Perhaps they might even register a momentary shift as one of the jars disappeared from the surface of the table before her, only to reappear a millisecond later in a slightly different position. Spot the difference, again and again.

But there was no observer. For when Rachel ate, she ate alone.

Bit by bit, the landscape of food before her was eroded. Mountains became hills, peaks fell into gentle slopes, which in turn, gave way to level plains. The resulting effect resembled the sped-up replaying of time-lapse photography. An entire roast turkey was picked clean by invisible hands, its gray, fatty bones emerging piecemeal from behind cooked flesh as though the bird was performing some kind of macabre striptease. In a matter of seconds, color began to drain away from the multi-colored feast before her; the tide of food was going out, leaving only a shoreline of bone-white china in its wake.

Finally, her refueling nearly complete, Rachel slowed the movements of her arms down to merely human speeds. Her smoky limbs flickered and strobed above the table as they solidified back into sight. With one trembling hand, Rachel reached for a tall glass filled with a glutinous, yellow liquid. She downed the pint of cooking oil in one gulp, then wiped the dregs of fat from her lips with the back of one hand. She paused for a moment as if in thoughtful contemplation, then yawned wide as a shuddering belch forced its way up from deep within her, the gassy noise shockingly loud in the quiet confines of her modest Ealing flat.

The woman known professionally as China Doll pushed herself back from the table, a grossly distended stomach poking out from beneath her nightdress like some monstrously overdue pregnancy. On unsteady legs, she rose and began the onerous task of clearing away the table.

She'd need to make some space for dessert, after all.

* * *

The brightly-colored heroes danced across Rachel's television screen in an explosion of comic-book violence. Roundhouse punches and high-stepping kicks were thrown with wild abandon, transforming a parade of cookie-cutter criminals into so many human-shaped punching bags. And yet, despite the ferocity of the blows, the camera was careful to never linger too long on anything truly upsetting. A broken arm here, a spray of dislodged teeth there, and yet the participants' injuries rarely appeared to be life-threatening. In fact, it almost looked fun.

As for the heroes, their carefully choreographed movements seemed designed merely to highlight their own overblown physiques. Each punch was an excuse for another struck pose, each tumbling kick merely the means to showcase their agility and prowess. The male and female superheroes were exaggerated caricatures of their sex: the men with muscles bulging like steroid abusing bodybuilders, the women with surgically enhanced busts that appeared to defy both gravity and sense. Clad in skin-tight Lycra and plunging necklines, their costumes seemed designed more to reveal than protect. Posing pouches drew the eye towards unfeasibly bulging male crotches, whilst the women seemed unperturbed by fighting in nine-inch high stiletto heels. Each hero seemed untouched by the violence around them—not a solitary hair out of place, not a single smudge of their carefully applied make-up.

Bastards.

Rachel McFarland hated the superheroes on TV. She hated the pomp, the ceremony, the too-bright smiles and the too-even teeth. She hated the good-looks, the plastic fantastic, their fast cars and famous boyfriends. She hated their celebrity status, tie-in films, perfume brands and fawning fans. She hated the money, the jewellery, the adulation and the fame. But most of all she hated the fact that she wasn't one of them.

Bastards. Just look at them. Typical Americans. Swanning about like they owned the place, like they were better than everyone else. Like they were any better than her.

It was all the government's fault. Oh, it was fine if you happened to have powers and lived in the U.S.A. Then, fame and fortune could be yours for the taking. Heroes were appreciated there. More than that, they were idolized. But the British public could never bring themselves to celebrate anything as vulgar as success. A grudging respect for saving the odd life would be coupled with a sneering comment about the privileged few, and how much were they earning again? Never mind the fact that 90 percent of her salary went on taxes, a special charge designed to recoup the costs incurred by her parent's involvement in the metahuman program. Never mind the fact that she was a public servant charged with a duty to help keep her country safe. Nurses, teachers, firemen, police—they didn't have the luxury of swanky superpowers, they just got on with the job. No, the British reserved their admiration for the underdog, whilst the media fed that hunger by tearing people down in order to build them back up again. Maybe she should develop a debilitating drug habit, she thought, at least for a little while.

The ringing of the telephone distracted Rachel from her reverie, its sound immediately echoed by Buggalugs as he sang along in a wailing counterpoint. She cursed the cat under her breath and began to search amongst the accumulated clutter for her mobile, but the call died before she could locate it.

Buggalugs looked up accusingly at her from amongst the detritus of discarded food wrappers that infested the room like tangled plastic weeds. There had been an incident only last week when she had accidentally eaten five tins of his cat food (tuna chunks in rich jelly, yum yum), before her taste buds had even registered the mistake, and she still wasn't sure if the flea-bitten mongrel had forgiven her. God help her, but she'd have to tidy this place at some point.

Her morning meal complete, Rachel had gravitated to the living room, the call of the sofa impossible to resist. Strewn across its upholstered skin like a murder victim, she had nevertheless continued to graze, albeit at a more sedate pace. Eating at speed may free up more hours in the day, but if she ate too fast, she'd be burning off the very energy she was trying so hard to accumulate. '*With great power comes great appetite*' ought to be her motto, she thought grimly. How she envied all those heroes whose powers weren't so damnably rational, all those who derived their abilities from mystic rings, alien technology, or exposure to random quantum flaws in the structure of space-time. It was alright for them, but if Rachel wanted to soar across the sky or punch holes in the sides of buildings, she had to first ingest enough food to fuel that power. '*Energy cannot be created or destroyed, only converted.*' Bloody Einstein and his Law of Conservation.

The phone rang again, and Rachel honed in

on the sound, locating it with a squeal of triumph. It had been hiding in an empty crisp packet all the time. Typical. "Hello?"

The voice on the other end of the line was rich and smooth, like chocolate dipped in coffee. "Ah, Miss McFarland. I bring you greetings of death and destruction."

"And the same to you, Brains. How's it hanging?"

"I take it you haven't seen the television this morning?"

"I'm watching it now, actually. *American Justice Live*. Swish bastards."

"Try changing to BBC1, then."

Rachel flipped the channel, and the superheroic antics were replaced by shaky-cam footage of panicking civilians. The crowds were flooding down the stone steps of an imposingly large structure that Rachel found vaguely familiar. Sirens echoed the screams and cries of those caught up in the drama, whilst a hastily erected partition of policemen was attempting to hold back a line of doom-obsessed reporters who seemed intent on storming the building. "I dunno, it's some sort of disaster movie, I guess."

"Look again."

A dull *crump* punctuated the chaotic soundtrack, and fresh screams erupted as something was punted from an open doorway into the fleeing crowd. The mass of densely packed bodies sprung apart as though repelled by some invisible force, scattering every which way. The picture rushed to fill the rapidly emptying steps, panning from side to side until a small round object could be glimpsed between the confused tangle of legs. The object of its search located, the camera zoomed in still further, revealing the grisly details of a man's severed head. A smear of crimson stretched from it down the pavement, the blood and flesh combining into a macabre exclamation mark. One of the fleeing crowd accidentally caught the head a glancing blow as they passed and punted it across the street like a fleshy football. The cranium collided with a street lamp with a dull *crump*, and Rachel swallowed hard. The BBC would never tolerate a movie this gruesome to be broadcast before the watershed. Even news footage this explicit wouldn't be allowed. Not unless it was being broadcast live.

"Where is this?" she gasped.

"The Natural History Museum. South Kensington. It shouldn't take you long. The rest of the team are already on their way, Rachel, but I know you'll get there first. We'll meet you there."

Rachel let the phone fall from her hand. She was dressed and out of the door before it even had time to hit the floor.

Buggalugs registered the breeze of her hyperspeed departure with a sense of resigned frustration. Translated into human terms, his thoughts were simple: who's going to feed me now?

* * *

It wasn't flying as such, more like a series of extended leaps.

Rachel cut through the air at supersonic speed, the boom of her passing shattering upper story windows and overturning cyclists and pedestrians alike. Collateral damage, she thought. Let them file a claim against the department, like everyone else.

The angles of her bulky costume cut into her

flesh, but she was glad of its mass. Covered from the neck down in interlocking plates of toughened ceramic, the material protected Rachel from both enemy assault and unwanted press attention. As far as the world new, the armored powerhouse known as China Doll was Rachel's true form, with only a few carefully posed publicity photographs showing a glimpse of the woman beneath. What the tabloids didn't know was that the slim and attractive girl in the stills had been airbrushed to within an inch of her life: Rachel's true form—at least before she went into battle—was inevitably that of a bloated monster. Vast swathes of fat hung from her at the start of any given mission, the mass carefully hidden behind obfuscating layers of painted ceramic. When expending energy at a superhuman rate, the resulting chemical reaction inevitably led to a massive increase in body temperature. For Rachel, the phrase 'burning off fat' was all too literal, and the last thing she needed was some paparazzi catching a glimpse of the gruesome process going on inside her. She could already feel the inner plates of her armor beginning to warm as she raced above the streets of London, and a smell uncomfortably like that of cooking bacon began to waft up from within. Trying not to gag, Rachel relaxed her muscles, the better to pace her energy expenditure, and concentrated on her shoulder mounted SatNav.

With every second, the mass of London's Natural History Museum loomed larger against the skyline. The museum's extravagant structure was a vibrant splash of color against the surrounding mass of anonymous white-walled buildings, the patchwork of its multi-hued brickwork shining brightly in the midday sun. As she neared, Rachel could make out a series of stone figures perched proudly above the museum's many windows, gargoyles and pterodactyls alternating like opposing figureheads of superstition and science.

A cordon had been set up along Exhibition Road, with the flashing lights of emergency vehicles marking the dividing line between police and public. Several of the police officers were carrying guns, their black armor-clad forms resembling giant sinister beetles. Rachel aimed her flight towards the back of a van where a group of these figures were clustered thickly. The force of her landing sent most of the police to their knees, but one grizzled veteran had the presence of mind to brace himself against the van's open doors. Rachel recognized him vaguely. Another day, another crisis. "What's the situation here?" she barked, hoping that the light breeze would quickly disseminate the smell of her gently roasting flesh.

The policeman gagged but quickly recovered. "All I know is that there's something inside that's killing people, Miss. I'll radio Captain Hunt and let him know you've arrived. He's got a squad inside, and I believe one of your colleagues is already with him."

"Oh, excellent news. I hate dying alone."

* * *

Away from the muggy summer heat and the panicked crowds, the interior of the Natural History Museum was an eerie oasis of calm. Rachel could still make out the vague sounds of humanity outside, but it all seemed so distant, as though the crisis that gripped the populace was taking place elsewhere in the capital. Deprived of the usual milling throng, the museum had taken on the air of a deserted church, an unlikely setting for a scene of violent demise. Bloody bodies lay strewn across its marble floor, their languid forms scattered like so many broken dolls. Uncaring and remote, the dead reclined in apparently peaceful repose, the exhausted remnants of a finished fight.

Rachel picked her way gingerly through the destruction, as though careful not to wake the sleeping dead. The corpses were clumped thickest about a giant dinosaur skeleton that dominated the main hall, the bodies tangled up around its four legs like debris caught up in a flowing stream. The hundred-foot-long skeleton loomed over them like some avatar of death, and Rachel had a sudden image of the long-extinct creature returning to life for one brief moment of revenge against the species who had supplanted it. Ridiculous, but then what *had* caused this amount of carnage?

As Rachel stepped past the posed skeleton and further into the hall, she realized she was not the only person still standing. A young girl had her back to Rachel, her attention fixed on the debris around her. She appeared to be about twelve years old, a school blazer and skirt indicative of her youth. Several of the girl's classmates lay about her, their spindly limbs jutting up at odd angles from the floor as though they were cruelly crushed insects.

Hearing Rachel's approach, the girl whipped her pig-tailed head around and fixed her with wet, doleful eyes. "Please, Miss, I can't find my Mummy. Could you help me?"

Rachel sighed. "Quit the theatrics, Lucy. You're one sick kid, you know that?"

Rachel's teammate giggled, and the glistening pink skin of bubblegum burst in her mouth with a loud pop.

"Couldn't you save *any* of these people?" Rachel asked.

Lucy shrugged and pointed to the corduroy-clad form of a man who had been embedded face first into one of the museum's walls. His cranium had completely flattened under the force of the impact, bursting apart like a ripe fruit. "Look at Mr. Geoffrey, there," sighed Lucy. "Squished like a bug. Such a shame. I never did like History."

"You're all heart, Luce. What did all this?"

"I'm not sure *what* it was, but I can tell you it sure as hell wasn't friendly. The rest of the class didn't stand a chance. Tragic, really. Just think—if we get this wrapped up quick enough I'll probably get the rest of the day off school."

Rachel sighed. "That's right—always look on the bright side of life, Lucy. So, where is this thing now?"

"Some of the guys from Special Ops have got it contained in the basement. This way, China Doll."

Rachel followed the schoolgirl through an alcove at the rear of the hall, then along a series of twisting corridors that led deeper into the museum. A parade of stuffed animals stared glassy-eyed at them as they passed. Eventually, the display cases made way for the blank whitewashed walls of areas out of bounds to the general public. Lucy halted at an anonymous wooden door surrounded by police, their armored forms bristling with radio antennae and unholstered guns. Out of place amongst them crouched an elderly man in a tweed jacket, a shock of frizzy white hair framing his weather-beaten face. The elderly man turned to face them as they approached, his actions mirrored by the most senior of the police. Rachel recognized the moustachioed figure of Captain Hunt from previous assignments and briefly nodded her head in greeting.

"Good evening, gentlemen," announced Lucy, cheerfully. "We are your government sanctioned superheroes, or at least those that aren't caught up in the London traffic. My name is Lucy Tuesday, and this armor-clad cutie beside me is Rachel McFarland, though you probably know us better as 'Little Miss Pester' and 'China Doll.' We are here to save your asses by kicking someone else's. Violently. So let's get to it."

"Yes, ma'am." Captain Hunt snapped off a quick salute and inclined his head towards the door behind him. "We have the creature holed up in the research labs downstairs. That's where it first broke free according to Professor Summers here."

"This true, old man?" Lucy asked the Professor. "What exactly are we dealing with here?"

"I don't know that I care for your tone, young lady," the Professor bristled, clutching his lapels manfully. "I don't have to tell you anything."

"Professor Summers," cut in Rachel wearily, "if you know who Lucy Tuesday is, you'll know that you *will* tell her whatever she wants to know, whether you like it or not. So just cut out the crap and tell us now."

Professor Summers appeared to consider his options for a moment, before submitting to the inevitable. "Well . . . whatever it is down there, just remember that it belongs to the British Museum, alright? I'm well aware of your people's reputation for wanton destruction, but I would like to remind you that this is a valuable historical artifact, and not some costumed super villain for you to beat up or throw into the sun."

Rachel sighed. "Professor, it may have escaped your notice, but your precious historical artifact has already killed upwards of a dozen people. Now stop stalling and tell us exactly what we're dealing with."

Summers harrumphed indignantly before continuing. "It is, or rather it was, a person. A man to be precise. What happened was this. A sarcophagus was uncovered at an archaeological dig in Egypt a few weeks ago. The tomb appeared to be nearly two thousand years old, and scans indicated that the sarcophagus contained a well-preserved body. So, we had it shipped back to England for examination. And then, well . . . "

"Revenge of the Undead Mummy from Hell?" Lucy cut in. "Ho-lee shit."

"Hang on a minute," said Rachel. "This isn't the Victorian Age. Why did you bring the remains back to England anyway? Won't the Egyptians be a bit miffed at you stealing one of their historical treasures?"

"Well, they might be," admitted Professor Summers, "if it was one of theirs. However, hieroglyphics in the tomb indicated that the inhabitant wasn't Egyptian at all. In fact, he's British."

"What? So let me get this straight—you bring home a *British* mummy that was buried in Egypt two thousand years ago, then it comes to life and starts killing everybody in sight?"

"That's perfectly correct, Miss McFarland."

"Terrific, Professor. Just terrific." Rachel pushed her way past the armed police and shouldered open the wooden doors, revealing a narrow staircase leading down into stygian depths. "What happened to the lights down here?"

"I turned them off earlier," said Lucy, "It's creepier this way. C'mon people, let's go."

* * *

The police led the way downstairs, the beams of their flashlights cutting though the darkness like gleaming swords. Professor Summers directed their movements from the rear, ushering them through a series of dismal rooms until the group arrived at what he referred to as 'the place of disinterment.'

The policemen played their flashlights over the contents of the room, gradually bringing indistinct shapes into focus. The rectangular space was lined with shelves, where clusters of scientific instruments huddled against each other like mechanical pets. The room was dominated by a waist-high bench upon which was laid a huge open coffin, its painted sides partially covered by protecting wraps of cloth.

Rachel moved closer to the sarcophagus, eager for a glance inside the hollow shell, only to find herself stumbling over something underfoot. "Whoops. Light, please, somebody?"

Captain Hunt obliged, and Rachel took an involuntary step back as she saw she was standing in the wet remains of what had once been a human being. The body seemed almost unrecognizably mangled, but Professor Summers stifled a gasp as he pushed his way forward. "It's Matthews!" he cried. "Poor old Matthews. Well, poor young Matthews actually. He only joined us last month. He was working on his degree. But now look at him!"

"I would if I could, Professor," said Rachel,

"but, is it me, or is it getting darker in here?" Rachel gazed in growing alarm at the bobbing flashlights that stabbed through the murky gloom. Surely there should be five lights, not four? Had someone's batteries failed? She started to count the criss-crossing beams of light again, but now there only appeared to be three. "I hate to break it to you guys," she said quietly, "but I don't think we're alone in here."

Rachel turned towards Captain Hunt, but he was gone. A muffled gasp, a sound of snapping bone, and the room was plunged into total darkness.

"Professor, are you still there?" Lucy's high-pitched voice cut through the inky blackness, and Summers grunted something in reply. "Because there's something I've been meaning to ask you about this mummy. You say it belongs to the British Museum, and that makes sense, of a sort, because they have a whole section on Ancient Egypt. But why bring it across town to the Natural History Museum? They haven't even got any mummies here— just animals and rocks and stuff. It doesn't make any sense."

Summer's disembodied voice floated out of the darkness. "Because we were told to."

"Told to? By whom?"

The Professor grunted but held his tongue.

"You'd better answer me, Prof, or I'll use my power on you. I mean it." The silence was deafening. "OK then," Lucy sighed, "you asked for it."

Rachel began to feel dizzy as she heard Lucy chanting in the darkness. *TellMeTellMeTellMe-TellMe*—Lucy's words ran together into one seamless unending command, speeding up to an impossible rate, the words repeated millions of times a second in the same hypnotic, droning, schoolgirl voice. As bad

18

as the side effects felt for Rachel, they would be unimaginably worse for Professor Summers. Tests had shown that the targets of Lucy's 'pester power' had reported time itself seeming to warp under the strain of her demands, with each second extended into an agony of hours. Under such a sustained barrage of pestering, grizzled bank robbers would throw down their loot, rabid terrorists throw down their guns, and diverse nightmarish villains would sink to their knees in submission—*anything* to be rid of the nightmare little girl whose voice whined on, and on, and on, and on . . .

Professor Summers started coughing, his voice forcibly dragged up through his throat despite his best efforts to resist. "Hnnn. It. Hnnn. It was. Hmmm. It was . . ." Professor Summers choked back a sob in the darkness as something forced its hand over his mouth. "Mmmph. Gumphh." A sound like a snapping turkey bone echoed through the darkness, and Professor Summers spoke no more.

Rachel remained stock still as Lucy's chant faltered, her eyes wide for any hint of movement within the unending black. And then, she found that she *could* see, but only dimly, a faint blue luminescence that seemed to be emanating from somewhere on the floor. Emanating from—

"Matthews! Good God, Lucy—look at Matthew's body!"

The crumpled corpse of the ex-scientist was glowing with an eerie blue light, the flickering phantasmal glow sending out a fitful illumination into the room. As Rachel watched, the corpse slowly began to move, its splintered limbs stirring as though it was being manipulated by unseen hands. As if waking from a deep slumber, the body shuffled itself into a sitting position before letting out a weary moan. "Abase yourselves insects. Abase yourselves before our undying master!"

Rachel shuddered. "Lucy, are you doing that? I didn't know your power could affect the dead."

"It can't. It's not me, Rachel. I don't know who's doing this!"

Matthews's corpse opened its mouth wider, a hoarse shout issuing from between his ruined lips. "He comes! The immortal king has risen—all hail the Undying King!"

The cadaver repeated the phrase, and soon the lone voice became a chorus. The eerie blue light waxed, rushing to fill the corners of the room as the crumpled bodies of Professor Summers, Captain Hunt and his men rose from where they had recently fallen. Each person's neck had been snapped, their heads now hanging boneless and slack upon blood-ied breasts, but still their voices came.

"Who?" Rachel shouted desperately. "What King? Where?"

Rachel and Lucy pressed closer as the undead shuffled forward, their attention fixed so firmly upon the nightmare unfolding before them that they paid little heed to what was occurring elsewhere. It was only when Lucy screamed that Rachel became aware of the presence above them both, a confused tangle of unfurling limbs that dropped down upon Lucy like a yo-yo before bearing its prize back to its perch.

Rachel snapped her head upwards, trying to make sense of what she was looking at. Wedged amongst the rafters, like an overgrown spider, was the figure of a man, his ancient skin pitted and cracked like old leather. Tongues of blue fire lapped from the creature's empty eye sockets, whilst its mouth hung open in a slack and boneless grin. About its abdomen hung a succession of musty bandages, the partially removed wrappings hanging in baggy folds like loops of disgorged intestine. The gigantic figure clutched the struggling Lucy to its chest like a doll, the young girl's efforts having little effect against the monstrous creature. Lucy began to intone frantically, the rapid repetitions of '*PutMeDownPutMeDownPutMeDown*' audible from where Rachel stood, but no sooner had she begun than the mummy held her by one leg and swung her casually to one side. Lucy's head connected with a ceiling beam with a resounding *thunk*, and she instantly fell silent. The mummy shook the girl experimentally for a moment, as if testing a broken toy for signs of life, before contemptuously hurling it aside.

"Bastard!" Rachel felt the adrenalin rush and before she had time to think she was moving. Traveling at near supersonic speed, she burst from the clutches of the advancing dead, her momentum carrying her off the ground in a crude semblance of flight. Both fists extended, she powered into the creature above, her ceramic-sheathed body connecting with a satisfyingly solid impact. The air was suddenly thick with a sickly sweet stench as rotten breath was forced from the vile thing's lips. The monster was doubled up, and making use of her advantage, Rachel kicked the winded monster between the legs as hard as she could. She had no idea whether mummies actually possessed testicles or not, but she felt a sense of satisfaction as the creature toppled sideways from its perch and crashed to the ground below. "That one's for you, Lucy!"

Feeling her body burning with expended energy, Rachel dropped, her legs extended for impact on the creature below, but the creature suddenly flipped onto its back and scuttled out of harm's way. Damn, that thing was fast!

Before Rachel had a chance to pull herself to her feet, the undead figures of Summers, Hunt and the rest were upon her. Blows rained down about her as the bloody creatures used their own limbs as crude bludgeoning implements. Most of the blows landed ineffectually against her ceramic armor, but Rachel smelt burning flesh as one zombie reached for her unprotected face. The corpse immediately howled as its fingers began to melt against her burning hot skin and she shoved it backwards violently. The skin on the tips of the zombie's fingers remained fused upon her, stretching and pulling like taffy, until it appeared that a long pink elbow glove stretched incongruously between the pair. With a squeal of disgust Rachel reached up an armored hand, pulled the fleshy extrusion of skin from her face, and snapped it back at her attacker like a giant elastic band. Following through, she punched the zombie's head clean off its shoulders and began to take apart the remaining reanimated dead with the grim determination reserved for an unpleasant but necessary chore.

The blue fire that washed over the dead lent them an unnatural strength, but it was no match for Rachel's own. Within seconds, the dead were reduced to a quivering collection of disparate body parts and Rachel turned her attention to the bandage-wrapped figure that had directed their assault. "Your turn now, big fella!"

The mummy let out a wordless shriek and turned away from her, punching an exit through the far wall with its glowing blue fists. Rachel followed through falling debris of brick and mortar, only to find the creature already punching another exit in the far wall of the next room. She chased the mummy as it tore its way through a succession of rooms, a series of stored artifacts, dusty paperwork and maintenance pipes flitting past her vision like blurry snapshots.

Rachel was dimly aware of the words 'Darwin Center' flashing past her as the creature led her upstairs and into an annex of the main building. Compared to the faux-medieval style of the museum proper, the multi-level cocoon she now found herself in was shockingly modern. Pickled organisms hung suspended in glass, their variegated forms displayed against clinically stark backgrounds. Against the ordered lines of modernity, the mummy looked even more like a relic from the past, a shambling nightmare from the golden age of Hollywood, thrust out of its natural habitat. The creature seemed confused and paused at the foot of a collection of giant spirit jars, before turning to face its pursuer.

Rachel took two steps towards the creature, readying herself for a final showdown, when she became aware of two curious things.

The first was the man. He was standing nonchalantly to one side of the display area, seemingly unperturbed by the fact that a walking, mummified corpse had just been pursued into the area by a ceramic armored superhero. The man appeared to be in his mid-thirties and was short in stature, standing no more than five foot in height. He was clad in the bowler hat, and suit and tie of a stereotypical London banker, an effect which was spoiled somewhat by the mirrored sunglasses perched incongruously upon his nose. On noticing Rachel's attention, the man gave a slight bow of his head, as if he was one professional acknowledging another, then tipped his hat, smiling all the while.

The second thing Rachel noticed was Archie, bobbing gently in his tank. Of course, she could hardly have failed to notice the presence of the Center's most famous exhibit, as the pickled monstrosity dominated the room. She'd seen the animal before, having watched the unveiling of the eight-and-a-half meter long giant squid on the news last summer. She remembered being shocked at the creature's sheer scale, awed at the huge trailing limbs depending from its swollen sack of a body, and amused by the inappropriateness of giving an exotic beast such a mundane nickname.

What she couldn't remember was the pale blue glow limning the creature's hide, nor the way it bobbed and rolled in its glass tank like a drowning man. The reanimated mummy threw its arms aloft, and the blue flames within its eye sockets burned with a brighter intensity. The squid followed suite, its body now bathed in the same unearthly glow, the preserving alcohol that surrounded it suddenly beginning to boil.

The next instant the giant squid's eyes flicked open and one rubbery limb smashed forward. The tank exploded outward in a hail of glass and a flood of preserving fluid gushed out upon the museum floor. The squid was borne forward upon the crest of a stinking alcoholic wave, and before Rachel had time to think, Archie was upon her. Its tentacles thrashed at her like giant snakes, the muscular limbs pulling at the seams of her suit until they split under the strain. Piece by piece, the plates of ceramic armor were ripped free, laying segments of Rachel's burning red flesh bare. Rachel had a sudden image of the squid as a diner enthusiastically plucking at the carapace of a still living lobster and recognized the oncoming rush of giddy hysteria. Her reddened flesh burned at the giant squid's touch, but the sensation seemed to inflame the creature all the more, and it pulled at her with renewed vigor.

Rachel choked for breath as the dead animal hugged her in its rubbery embrace, spluttering from the disgorged preserving fluid that washed about her. She tried to free her arms but they were pinioned tight to her sides. There was nothing she could do. Somewhere in the distance she could hear a dusty hacking cough, and she realized dimly that the re-animated mummy was laughing at her. She knew the thought should have enraged her, but it was so difficult to care anymore. Better to just slip quietly beneath the waves.

Rachel was on the edge of unconscious-ness when a new sound cut through the mental fog. Breaking glass, followed by a man's voice. "Have no fear—Mr. Oleaginous is here!"

And suddenly she was wet again, soaked from head to foot in a substance whose nature she really didn't wish to dwell upon. The pressure of Ar-chie's tentacles began to decrease as she felt the gi-ant squid struggle to retain a hold of its now slippery prey. Suddenly, there was the comforting sensation of human arms about her, and there was Oliver Ran-garajan—her hero—holding her tight, the only man who could get a grip through the superhuman waves of moisture that leaked from his own pores. Ollie's super-sweat had a particularly gnarly tang this after-noon, like an athlete's plimsoll marinating in a buck-et of warm goat's milk, and Rachel tried to tell her-self that this really *was* preferable to being crushed to death by a zombie sea monster from Hell. Lubed to the max, Mr. Oleaginous and China Doll popped from Archie's tentacled grasp like a cork from a wine bottle, the pair of them sliding across the floor in a wide stripe of bodily fluids before coming to a halt at the far wall.

Rachel looked up at her teammate and rescuer, his podgy glistening body naked except for a pair of eye-wateringly tight silver Lycra shorts and matching utility belt. "Oliver Rangarajan, *please* tell me you're going to get a better catch-phrase than that."

A mournful voice came from over Ollie's shoulder. "I know. Pathetic, isn't it? And you didn't even mention me, Ollie. I can feel one of my pouts coming on, I really can."

Oliver cast a wry smile at Rachel, then stepped to one side, revealing a brooding man dressed in a long leather coat. "As if you hadn't already guessed, Rachel, may I announce the presence of none other than Mr. Michael Chance himself."

"I would rather you announced me by my professional moniker, if you please, Mr. Oleaginous," said the figure. "It is not for nothing that I am known the depth and breadth of the land as The Incredible Sulk."

"Hang on," replied Oliver. "Isn't that a copyright infringement? Brains told me they put an injunction against you."

Michael pouted. "Don't make me sorry, Ollie. You wouldn't like me when I'm sorry."

Oliver slapped a sopping hand to his brow in mock despair. "Oh, you sad, sad bastard."

Suddenly, a thick, rubbery tentacle smashed between them like a falling tree, and the trio turned their attention back to the giant squid. The creature thrashed amidst the shattered remains of its tank, seemingly oblivious to the lack of water that would have sustained it in life. Using its limbs like grappling hooks, the creature began to haul itself closer to where the three superheroes waited. Arms extended in front of him, Oliver blasted a jet of stinging sweat across the creature's lumpish brow, but it came implacably on. "Where's Pester, anyway?" he asked. "Shouldn't she be here too?"

"Lucy's downstairs," gasped Rachel, still struggling to get her breathing back on an even keel. "I don't know if she's alive or dead, but she's out of this fight."

"Damn. It looks like this one's up to you then, Michael."

"I've told you before," Michael replied, "it's The Sulk. And because you have offended me so, I shall do absolutely nothing to aid you."

Michael thrust his hands deep into the pockets of his leather coat and cast his eyes into the middle distance in a pose of studied disinterest. Familiar with the routine, Rachel and Oliver edged themselves further back, putting as much distance between themselves and the pasty faced hero as possible. Sighing exaggeratedly, The Sulk removed a small piece of metal from one pocket and began to methodically file his nails, seemingly oblivious to the sound of slurping wet meat bearing down upon him. Finally, having covered the distance in a series of tentacular heaves, Archie slowly pulled itself aloft on quivering limbs, hung momentarily suspended above Michael's head—

"No. Nothing at all."

—before descending.

Michael disappeared into the creature's cavernous maw and with a sucking heave, Archie swallowed The Sulk whole.

"Bugger." Michael's voice was faint but still audible, his tones muted by layers of blubbery hide. "It smells bad in here, guys. *Really* bad. Worse than 'Mr. Oleaginous on a hot day' bad. No offence, Ollie."

"None taken."

The muffled voice began to take on a whining quality. "Oh, woe! Woe is me! Shunned by my teammates, misunderstood by my fans, and now interred alive in the belly of this noble lord of the sea. I shouldn't care, but I do. My problem is, I care too much."

"Oh my God!" Rachel shrieked. "He's going to do it! Look out, Ollie, get your earplugs in!"

Oliver pulled out a pair of silicon moulded earplugs from his utility belt and frantically jammed them home. Rachel's own pair seemed to have become lost in the fight, so she desperately used her hands to cover her ears. It kept the worst of the nausea at bay, but she could still feel the side effects of Michael's awful power as The Sulk began to sing a droning dirge from deep within the belly of the beast:

"It's hard when you're loved by everyone.
It's tough when you are universally adored.
If only I still had some laudanum,
I'd snooze all, my blues all, awa-ay!
Oh, Mother, don't look at me so scornfully,
Just because I drank all of your gin.
The fact is I've grown quite attached to me,
Though I still want to do myself in!"

The words continued in a similar pathetic

28

vein, but Rachel tried not to listen too closely. It wasn't so much the lyrics, but the haunting melody, the mournful tone, that hurt so much. Michael's singing voice echoed in harmony with the negative vibes that underlay the universal condition, resonating on a subatomic level to bring everything bad to the fore. Entropy, death, loneliness—these essential truths were Michael's stock in trade, and no one who had heard his awful song could remain unaffected. Rachel wondered vaguely if giant zombie squid even had ears in any conventional sense, but, from the evidence of her eyes, it mattered little.

Archie was convulsing, his entire body resonating in sympathy to the vibrations of The Sulk's depressing dirge. The tremors passed through the creature in shuddering waves of sorrow, making the voiceless animal appear as though it was going through a series of wracking sobs. Archie's eyes welled with tears, the glutinous material quivering like gone-off jelly. The shaking increased to epileptic proportions and a succession of jagged crevasses began to creep across the creature's hide like ground scored by an earthquake's passage. As the creature shook itself to pieces, Michael slowly emerged from within its cerulean guts, his face streaming with tears and brine. His song complete, The Sulk laid a comforting hand upon the shredded squid's body, and he bowed his head in sorrow. "Such a waste. Such a terrible waste. I'm sorry, Archie. I'm so, so sorry."

The mood was broken by the sound of one man clapping, and Michael turned to face the bowler-hatted observer. "OK, two questions: one, who the hell are you? And two, where the hell is my mummy?"

The man in the bowler hat smiled and spoke

with a rich American twang. "In answer to your questions, my friend, I am nobody. I am nothing. Ignore my presence, for I am not here, and I never was. As to the cadaverous gentleman dressed in antique burial wraps, he went that-a-way."

The small man pointed to a shattered window in the side of the honeycombed building, through which Mr. Oleaginous suddenly appeared, riding like a surfer upon the crest of a wave of his own sweat. "Sorry guys, but whilst you were busy with our fishy friend, the mummy skipped town. I followed him as best I could, but once he got mounted I just couldn't keep up."

"Mounted?" asked Rachel. "What did he do—ride out of here on a horse?"

"Not exactly, Doll."

"What do you mean?"

Oliver gulped. "Let me put it this way—one of our dinosaurs is missing."

SECOND COURSE:
Cold Cuts, Tongue And Sundry Other Dead Meat
(Serves Two)

The food was glorious, and Oliver said so.

"I'm glad you like it, Ollie," replied Rachel, laughing. "The food in here can be rather exotic."

"It's good, really. And I'm doubly grateful it's not a curry, believe you me."

"Not a fan of the spicy stuff then?"

Oliver sighed. "In moderation, perhaps. But that's the trouble. Just because I'm of Indian descent everyone seems to think that curries are all I eat. Look at that 'thank you' meal we had to sit through last week. Roast venison, juniper sauce and sweet potatoes for everyone else, but what did I get? Chicken Korma and poppadoms. I wouldn't mind, but it happens at every single official function we have to attend. And I'm British. Third generation. I've never even *been* to India."

Rachel smiled. "I know, Ollie, I sympathize. But they were trying to be nice to us. And considering the amount of damage we did to the Natural History Museum, I'm surprised they didn't just send out for fish and chips."

"Hey, don't knock chips," laughed Oliver. "I can do with all the grease I can get!"

"Ah yes, I was forgetting. Mr. Oleaginous is a slippery customer, isn't he?"

Oliver smiled sourly. "Unfortunately, that

31

rather goes with the territory."

Rachel paused a moment, mulling her wine with her next choice of words. "Tell me then, Oliver. Your power. Blessing or curse?"

Oliver considered for a moment. "A bit of both to be honest. I mean, I don't begrudge my parents taking place in the trials—they didn't know what they were going to end up with. And it *is* quite fun I suppose, flying all over the place, fighting monsters, saving the world. I just wish my powers didn't have to be so, I don't know . . . *gross*.

"I mean, this sweat that pours out of me. Sure, it comes in handy in a fight, but it's not much fun when I'm not working. I have to keep eating crap to keep my reserves filled up. Or at least I did. So I'm fat. I smell like a pig. And I've got the complexion of a fifteen-year-old." He smiled wryly. "I doubt if you know what I mean. I mean, look at you—you're gorgeous."

Rachel laughed. "Oh, a body like mine takes a lot of sacrifice, Ollie. My own powers are not entirely without their side effects. I don't think we're really so different—you and I."

"I just wish things were a bit easier, with— you know." Oliver broke eye contact, seeming to find something of great interest on his half-empty plate. "Girls. And stuff."

Rachel slowly eased herself up, and began to sidle around the circular booth to Oliver's side of the table. "Oh, I'm sure it's not as bad as all that. The right girl is out there for you somewhere, I'm sure." She sat down beside him and gently touched the back of his hand. "And maybe much closer than you think."

Oliver blushed, and tried to recover his bonhomie. "But anyway, listen to me going on, all doom and gloom. I'm beginning to sound like The Sulk."

Rachel pouted. "Don't say that. Poor Michael. All those good looks, all that adoration. It didn't do him any good in the end, did it?"

"No. It was a shock. I'm still trying to come to terms with what happened, to be honest."

"I know. But anyway. Things are looking up for you I hear. Rumors of opportunities across the pond? Apparently, you've caught the attention of a certain non-existent bowler-hatted gentleman. Congratulations."

Oliver winced. "Nothing has been finalized yet, Rachel. It could still be any one of us. Maybe even you."

Rachel waved a hand dismissively. "Nah, I'm not glamorous enough for the big league. Besides which, you're the one with the funky new powers. How are they working out by the way?"

"Oh, not so bad. I'm glad I no longer have to worry about eating so much fatty rubbish anymore. The power source is practically limitless, apparently. Something to do with tapping into all this hidden energy scrunched up in the higher dimensions. Invisible, but sat right here alongside us. I don't know all the details, you'd have to ask Brains for that. I must admit that there is one side effect I'm still having a little trouble getting my head around, though."

"Oh, yes? What's that?"

"Immortality."

* * *

After the fight at the museum, Rachel was tired, hungry, and smelled faintly of giant squid. The last thing she needed was Brains going all mysterious on her. "I'll explain everything later," the voice on the phone had crackled, "just meet me at Waterloo Station in one hour's time. We have a train to catch."

One brief shower later, Rachel sprinted onto the main concourse of London's largest railway station and instantly spotted her boss amongst the milling throng of workaday commuters. There was something to said for having a distinctive appearance, she supposed.

Douglas Fairfax—known professionally as Brainbox—could hardly have blended in with the crowd had he tried. His bearing was erect and proud, giving him the aspect of a nobleman stranded amidst the common herd, while his steel gray hair and pince-nez glasses failed to entirely disguise his aging movie star good looks. Combined with his old-fashioned tweed suit and enormous handlebar moustache, he appeared to be some relic of a bygone age, a piece of human flotsam dredged up from England's glorious past and cast adrift upon the tides of time.

What really set Douglas apart however, was the object that waited alongside him. In common with most of his fellow passengers, Fairfax was burdened with baggage. Uniquely, he was the only commuter who had to use his luggage to carry around his own brains.

Thanks to the government's genetic tampering, Douglas Fairfax's gray matter had simply grown too large for his head. Science's attempt to gift man with mental powers had been successful up to a point, but Douglas would never win any beauty contests now. The plates of Fairfax's skull were constantly teased apart by the merciless pull of stainless steel clamps, and from the resulting cleft in his crown, there now stretched a thick cord of glistening brainstem. This pink and gray rope extended down Douglas's back like some rubbery ponytail, whilst the engorged mass of the connected cerebral matter lay housed within a large glass container that stood alongside. Less a box and more a display case, the contents of this five-foot tall fish tank bore little resemblance to any recognizable human organs. Deviated far beyond the norm, Douglas's brain matter was now a collection of disparate, mutated parts. Cauliflower shaped whorls of gray-pink meat bathed together in a soupy broth of blood and cerebrospinal fluid. Just looking at it made Rachel feel queasy, and given the wide berth that most of the crowd were giving Douglas, she obviously wasn't alone in that regard.

Douglas was busy tapping away at the side of his tank, and Rachel was uneasily reminded of a child at an aquarium trying to attract the attention of the fish. He looked up as she approached, a guilty smile playing about his lips.

"Playing with yourself again, eh, Brains? This better be worth it."

"Ah, China Doll, there you are. Glad you could join us."

"Us?"

"Er . . . I mean me. Sorry." Douglas withdrew his hand from the side of his brain case and began to finger his moustache distractedly.

"Are you alright, Brains? Where's the rest of the team?"

"Oh, they've already boarded."

Rachel cast a glance at the massive departure board that loomed above them. "Which train are they on, then?"

"Ah, my apologies, Rachel. I only wanted to meet you here for the sake of convenience. The train we need is actually over the road. Westminster Bridge Road, to be exact."

Rachel frowned, puzzled. "What on Earth are you talking about? There is no train station on Westminster Bridge Road."

Douglas smiled. "Not now, there isn't. But there used to be. Follow me, m'dear." Douglas immediately began to move towards the exit, his exotic luggage trundling close behind him.

His brain-box was mounted on a platform from which depended a number of stubby steel legs, the steam-driven limbs rising and falling in a clanking mechanical ballet. Rachel couldn't help but notice the looks of horror that inevitably stole across the faces of those they passed and felt a wave of sympathy for Douglas' plight. "Couldn't you have put some sort of sheet over your luggage, Douggie?" she asked.

"Oh, I used to," Brains called back, his upper-class accent drifting behind him in a wake of Received Pronunciation. "Trouble was, when nobody could make out what was actually in there, they paid no mind to cutting me off and getting in m' way. Believe me, once you've had a couple of cyclists inadvertently drive over your brainstem you soon realize that repulsed but forewarned is by far the preferable option."

Rachel followed her colleague out of the station, marveling at how the crowds parted around the bizarre monstrosity as though pushed aside by invisible hands. "Where are we going, again?" she asked.

"Tell me, Rachel, how's your history?" Fairfax called over his shoulder.

"Bloody awful. Why?"

Fairfax sighed theatrically. "The wonderful thing about this city is that nothing is ever truly lost forever, just quietly forgotten about and built over. The most incredible things surround us every day, and yet most pass by in blissful ignorance. History *endures*, if we know where to look, just waiting for its chance to be uncovered."

"Are you talking about London or our mummified friend?"

"Very good. Both, really. Everything has its time."

"Am I to take it then, that you have tracked down this 'Undying King'?"

Douglas turned and smiled at her. "Oh, yes. And not only that, but I've got transport laid on." He came to a halt at a sentry line of bus stop, bollards and bins, behind which an anonymous low-roofed gray and brown building lurked in the shadows. Fly posters of last year's bands wallpapered the bricked-up frontage, whilst a disused telephone kiosk alongside appeared to have taken on a new lease of life as a public toilet.

"Very salubrious," said Rachel sarcastically.

Fairfax turned to face her, struggling to contain his exasperation. "It may look shabby now, but between 1902 and 1941 this was the site of a working railway terminal."

"What happened in 1941, then?" Rachel asked.

"The Germans did. A direct hit from the Luftwaffe destroyed it, and no one ever got round to rebuilding it. As such, this is an ex-railway station. Disused. Deceased. Until now, obviously. Listen." Fairfax beckoned Rachel closer, and she pressed an ear against the poster-covered wall. Dimly, she could hear the rumble of engines.

"Let's have a closer look, shall we?" Fairfax unlocked a rusty iron door and ushered Rachel inside.

* * *

The locomotive idled in the sidings, its machined features softened by a hazy shroud of puff. Although at rest, the train seemed impatient to Rachel, panting away in great huffs of steam like some monstrous metal dog. She followed Fairfax on board, helping to steady his brain-box as it minded the gap with a series of mechanical hops. No sooner were they aboard than the train sprang to life, the metal beast issuing a furious roar of whistling steam and grinding gears as it rapidly began to pick up speed.

The old fashioned carriage in which Rachel and Douglas found themselves was not entirely deserted. Four women lolled against each other in the faded leather seats opposite, as though deep in the arms of a drunken stupor. Their features were hidden beneath rough Hessian hoods, with only identically cut plain woven dresses giving a clue as to the nature of their sex. "Who are these women, Douglas?" whispered Rachel. "And where's the rest of the team?"

"It's a bit difficult to explain where the rest of the team are right now, but suffice to say they are closer than you might think. As to the identity of the ladies opposite—why don't you ask them yourself?"

Rachel leaned forward and gently lifted the hood of the figure nearest to her. The revealed face was slack and gray, like something that had been dredged up from the bottom of a lake. The woman's head hung to one side at a violently askew angle, and Rachel could see the thick hemp of a hangman's noose biting violently into her neck. Closed eyes rolled beneath puffed up eyelids, and the woman's dry lips worked like a suckling babe as the she tried to force breath up past the constricting cord.

"Don't bother. She doesn't need air," interjected Douglas, halting Rachel in her attempt to pry the noose from about the woman's neck. "She's already dead. They all are."

Rachel backed away from the lolling corpse and cast an inquiring look back at her colleague. Douglas' eyes were rolled up in his head, a sure sign that he was currently using his mysterious powers. "Miss Rachel McFarland, may I present the late Mrs. Edith Thompson and friends. Mrs. Thompson was hung by the neck until dead at Holloway Prison on the 9th of January 1923, for the crime of adultery."

"Since when was adultery a capital offence?"

"This was 1923, remember. And there were extenuating circumstances. The man Edith was having an affair with, a Mr. Frederick Bywaters, murdered Edith's husband in cold blood. Edith was found innocent of the actual murder but, nevertheless, justice had to be seen to be done against both parties. So, on one cold January morning in 1923, both Edith and her lover were executed—he for murder, she for adultery. In different prisons, they both met the drop at exactly the same minute past the hour. Synchronized swinging one might say. Almost romantic, don't you think?"

Rachel shivered. "Hardly. What's she doing here?"

"The same as us. Heeding the call."

Edith's eyelids fluttered open, and Rachel started at the flecks of blue fire that danced within. "That glow. It's the same as in those re-animated bodies in the museum, isn't it? That mummy—it's doing all this. But why?"

"I'm not entirely sure. But I have a nasty feeling our Undying King is building himself an army. He's certainly chosen the right spot for it, anyway."

"What do you mean?"

"Well, if you had the power to bring the dead back to life, where would you go?"

Rachel paused for a moment in thought. "A cemetery?"

"Correct. And he hasn't picked just any cemetery either."

"What do you mean?"

"Have you heard of Brookwood's?"

"Should I have?"

"Then you'll have to forgive me another history lecture. By the mid-nineteenth century, London was literally overflowing with corpses. They were quite simply running out of space to bury them all. So, the idea of a grand new cemetery was born, one vaster than any cemetery ever built before, large enough to hold all of London's dead, forever. The name of this great city of the dead was, appropriately enough, The London Necropolis, and it was situated in Brookwood, Woking. There are something like two-hundred and fifty *thousand* corpses buried in Brookwood Cemetery. Now, thanks to our mummified friend, we can consider all of them as potentially hostile."

Rachel gulped. "And this is where we're headed, right?"

"I'm afraid so. Emily took this trip a few years

before us. Her body was moved to Brookwood's in 1971, along with the mortal remains of three other women who had been executed at Holloway Prison."

Rachel paused to think a moment. "So what's she doing on this train *now*?" she eventually asked. "Why isn't she already there?"

Fairfax shrugged. "Time is all out of joint. That's how we managed to track down our mummified friend in the first place. He's left some severe localized reality distortion in his wake."

"So that's how you did it." Rachel laughed humorlessly. "Frankly, I'm not sure how you managed to lose track of a mummified corpse riding a thirty-foot tall dinosaur skeleton in the first place."

Douglas removed his glasses and began to polish them furiously. "Well, quite. But once we started getting reports that the Necropolis Line was up and running again, we swiftly put two and two together."

"So this whole train used to be laid on just for the cemetery's benefit, then?"

"Exactly. Due to its location on what was then the outskirts of London, a special railway line was constructed to carry both coffins and mourners out to the cemetery. After the war and the popularization of the motor car—well, what's twenty-five miles to travel for a good funeral? The station was never rebuilt, hence the train line falling into disuse."

"So, what you're telling me is that not only are the other passengers and corpses from out of the past, but *the train itself* no longer exists in our time? Oh God, I've just realized—we're riding on a Ghost Train aren't we? Literally."

"Oh yes." Douglas Fairfax smiled. "Fun, isn't it?"

* * *

Rachel had already emptied three snack machines at Waterloo Station, but the prospect of going to war against two-hundred and fifty thousand zombies made her feel ill prepared. She was going to need energy soon, and lots of it. As it was, she still felt fatigued from the earlier incident in the museum. "I don't suppose there's a food car on this train, is there?" she asked.

Fairfax expressed his doubts but admitted they had nothing to lose by exploring their surroundings. No sooner had Rachel agreed to his suggestion, than she began to regret it. Every other carriage that they came across seemed to be filled with the undead. They sat in neat rows, like workers engaged in a daily commute, their heads nodding in gentle sympathy with the motion of the train. Their bodies were in various states of disrepair, the mangled and torn sharing elbow room with those whose exhumed condition was only betrayed by the unhealthy pallor of their skin. Almost all were clothed in old-fashioned style. Boaters and bonnets, tweed jackets and ties, corsets and ankle-length dresses dominated, whilst several elderly-looking cadavers were ensconced within voluminous white cotton night-dresses, as though auditioning for the role of silent movie ghosts. Some wore the visible marks of their deaths, their blood having blossomed up through layers of clothing to be borne upon their breasts like vulgar ruby brooches. A few even revealed the causes of the underlying traumas, with embedded knife handles protruding incongruously from within crimson-soaked chests. One man appeared to have a golf club growing from the top of his cranium, the metal stalk ascending bizarrely from his partially caved-in skull. Another appeared to have lost his head altogether, with only a ruined red mess visible above the exposed grin of his lower jaw. The figure held a revolver in its lap, its fingers worrying constantly at the method of his suicide like restless worms.

As they passed, the dead seemed to sense their presence, turning their faces towards them like flowers seeking the sun. Their gazes were curiously blank however, with little display of any guiding intelligence. The corpses seemed sluggish, as though awakening from some long sleep, and Douglas opined that the closer the train got to Brookwoods, the stronger the Undying King's influence would become. His thoughts seemed to be borne out by the blue glow that wreathed the undead in a ghostly aura. At first a subliminal wash, the cerulean glow seemed to strengthen with every mile the train traveled.

The most animated cadavers that Rachel and Douglas came across turned out to be the drivers, a tag-team of corpses bathed in the unearthly glow that emanated from the roaring blue inferno of the engine. One of the corpses looked to have been stitched back together from numerous disparate parts, his naked body an interlocking jigsaw of fleshly nubs and spigots.

Having been disturbed by the efforts of Douglas to maneuver his brains through the narrow door, the patchwork creature paused in its stoking of the ghostly fire and introduced both himself and his companion under the name William. "This is our train, in fact, sir," drawled the corpse in a thick Scottish accent. "'specially chartered, and all. All this cargo belongs to our boss now."

"And what cargo would that be, William?" hazarded Douglas.

"Why corpses, of course!" the dead thing laughed. "Old Knoxie'll be beside himself at seeing this amount of stiffs!"

Douglas laughed delightedly. "Ah, you are referring to Dr. Robert Knox, am I correct?"

"Right you are, sir. To be honest, my head's a bit queer at the moment, but Knoxie is a resident of Necropolis City these days, that much I do know. He moved down from Edinburgh when things got a bit too hot for him back home."

"Oh, I'll just bet he did." Fairfax raised an imaginary hat to the two corpses. "Mr. Burke, Mr. Hare. An honor to make your acquaintances, sirs."

* * *

Having searched the train in vain from end to end, one thing still puzzled Rachel. "You said the rest of the team were already on board, but I can't find them anywhere. Where are they, Brains?"

Douglas Fairfax paused a while he considered his answer, stroking his enormous moustache with an idle finger as though seeking inspiration within its bristly depths. "It's hard to explain, but it's all to do with time. As I said, this Undying King fellow is leaving a trail of time distortion in its wake. It's pulling all these bodies from back out of their respective time streams, and causality is buckling under the strain. Events are no longer quite as linear as they should be.

"This train for instance. It's here, and yet it's not here, depending on which way you look at it. It's only due to my own psychic abilities that I'm able to synchronize the pair of us with the ebb and flow of the tangled timestreams. Alone, you might be able to sense some strange things occurring, but I doubt if you'd be able to interact quite so intimately with objects from the past.

"And working in the fourth dimension *is* doing some very strange things to my brains though, I have to say. I seem to have memories of having come here already, with you, with the rest of the team. I feel like I've ridden this train before. But they don't feel like normal memories, if that makes any sense. It's almost as if they are memories of events which are still happening now."

While Fairfax had been talking, Rachel had been keeping an eye on the view outside. As the train had been cutting a path through a wooded glade, shards of sunlight had been glittering off something pacing them in the bordering trees. As the foliage thinned, Rachel began to make out the form of a second train running alongside them, the sun reflecting off of its polished metal and glass. Smoke puffed from the steam engine's chimney in gusts of blue haze as the second train constantly punched its way through its own exhaust. "I don't want to alarm you, Douglas, but there appears to be another train outside. It seems to be matching our speed."

Douglas Fairfax peered over his brain-box, craning his neck for a better view. "That's not another train, Rachel. I think it's this one. Look closer at the carriage directly opposite."

"Oh my God!"

Gazing back at them from the window of the opposite carriage was the mirror image of Douglas himself. The doppelganger faced himself across a gap of fifty feet, his appearance and pose identical to that of the man beside her. The only thing that assured Rachel that the image opposite was not merely a reflection was the identity of the person stood next to him in her place. "Look! It's Ollie!" Rachel wound down the window. "Mr. Oleaginous! Over here!"

"I'm not sure if he can hear you, Rachel," said Douglas, having moved to the far side of the carriage. "Just look out of the other side."

Rachel turned and faced the opposite window. "Is that—us?"

A third train matched their progress on the right. The inhabitants of this train had their backs to them as they gazed out of the far window of their own carriage, but Rachel had little difficulty in recognizing herself and Douglas. "I don't understand, Brains. Why are we here and over there?"

"I told you, m'dear, time's out of whack. And time and space *are* relative after all. The Earth spins, the universe expands. Adjust the location of something in time, and you adjust its relative location in space. We are here and there, both now and then."

Rachel felt a sudden itch in the back of her head, as though someone was watching her. She began to turn her head and noticed as she did so, that her time-displaced aspect in the carriage opposite was mirroring her movements. Rachel gasped in shock as she turned fully around. Standing directly in front of her was yet another image of herself. The effect was as though someone had silently erected a full length mirror behind her while her back had been turned. She screamed, and her duplicate's mouth yawned wide in matching terror.

"Look out!" she heard Douglas yell from somewhere. "We've nearly reached our destination. The timelines are converging!"

Rachel's duplicate was drawing inexorably closer, like a lover moving in for a kiss. As her mirrored features filled her vision, she whipped her head violently sideways, spinning away in a desperate attempt to avoid her own touch. Rachel stumbled back down the carriage, but wherever she turned, she was faced with multiple overlapping versions of herself, all seemingly inexorably drawn towards her as though compelled by magnetic force. She caught glimpses of her teammates through the crowd, multiple versions of Brainbox, Mr. Oleaginous and The Sulk passing over and through each other like insubstantial ghosts. The internal dimensions of the carriage itself seemed to be multiplied, the seats, lights and walls blurring as numerous overlays of dislocated realities fought for dominance. With nowhere left to run to, Rachel cowered against the shifting floor. Aspects of herself fell down upon her like rain, and she closed her eyes against the oncoming storm.

As it was, it took her several moments to realize that the hand upon her shoulder was not her own, but Douglas'. "Open your eyes, Rachel. We've arrived."

Rachel raised her head from the floor of the train and looked up at her teammates as they gathered themselves from similar positions. The heroes were dusting themselves down, preparing for the upcoming fight. Thankfully, there was now only one of each. They were unique again. Unstoppable, Rachel thought. Just look at them.

Douglas Fairfax—Brainbox—smiling confidently, sure of his superior knowledge and powers. Unflappable and indefatigable.

Oliver Rangarajan—Mr. Oleaginous—already stripping off his outer garments, his nut-brown flesh oiled up and ready to roll.

Michael Chance—The Sulk—stifling a yawn as he hunched deeper into his long leather coat, his brooding countenance the only external sign of the awful power that lurked within his breast.

They could do this. They could win. She was sure of it.

And then she looked outside.

As far as she could see, bodies. They stood at attention, limned in blue fire, packed in side by side like zombie sardines. The platform and the surrounding glade were awash with corpses, yet as she watched, a channel suddenly opened up within the sea of the dead. An opening. An invitation.

The four living humans departed the train and began to walk along the path of the dead.

* * *

At first, Rachel could see nothing but corpses. The silent rank and file pressed close about her, their unfocused eyes and slack jawed grins giving them an air of imbecilic menace. The flicking blue aura washed about the dunderhead dead, its ghost light painting their partially denuded frames in washes of eerie fire.

As with those on the train, the cadavers were in various stages of disrepair. Some looked freshly turned from the earth's embrace, while others were little more than shredded scraps of meat and bone. These last were more than clothed by the animating light: the cerulean haze seemed to be acting as a second supernatural skin, holding their bones together in a thin and gauzy embrace. Young and old, male and female, in parts or in whole, the one common factor amongst the varied dead was a certain absence of intelligence about the eyes. Whatever was directing these creatures, it was no longer the souls of those who had once worn these skins.

At length, Rachel turned her attention away from the aspects of the dead and towards the fleshy path that their bodies described. A steepled roof loomed above the serried ranks of the indecently departed, and Rachel realized that she and her companions were being herded towards a church. It was an impressive but slightly decrepit affair, with an air of thoughtless neglect evident in the stains of thick dust and broken glass that peppered its Gothic shell. Creeping vines threaded its pale gray walls like veins, the discolored stone echoing the necrotic complexions of the milling congregation. Rachel, Douglas, Michael and Oliver felt the touch of cold hands upon them and, in an obscene reversal of a funeral procession, the dead ushered the living up a flight of broad stone steps and into the church itself.

Out of the bright midday sun, the interior was dark and cool. It took Rachel's eyes a few moments to adjust to the contrast, then the blurred shapes before her began to take on a horrible clarity. Every aisle was full, the assembled horde of the dead turning as one to face the living intruders. Their combined gaze was unsettling enough, but Rachel's attention was swiftly claimed by the figure that perched spider-like upon the altar.

Its wrappings were now mostly absent, with only a thick central mass remaining about the creature's abdomen, but there was no mistaking the ghoulish face of the mummy from the museum. Blue fire still flickered about the creature's sockets, but now they bled around the sides of a pair of shriveled, poached egg-like eyes.

On the marbled floor at the foot of the altar lay the remains of a young man, his slender frame clad in rich garments. A shallow nimbus of blood glistened wetly around the youth's body, the stub of an embedded knife protruded obscenely from his chest. As Rachel watched, a glow of blue fire blossomed from within the corpse like embers flaring in a breath of air, and the boy's chest began to rise and fall. Uttering a series of pitiful moans, the dead youth drew himself slowly up to his knees, pulling all the while at the handle that protruded from him. Breathing heavily, the boy plucked the dagger from his breast inch by inch, and a smile stole briefly across his features.

No sooner had he done so however, than the mummified corpse upon the altar reached down, wrapped one leathery hand about the boy's own, and plunged the still gripped knife back into his chest. The boy screamed and sank back down onto the floor, his body slowly stilling as the blue flame of life flickered and died.

The mummified cadaver chuckled to itself, then turned to address the group of heroes in a wheezing, groaning voice. "Tell me . . . do you know who this was?"

Rachel struggled to find her voice, but an unintelligible grunt was all that emerged.

"His name was Edward," the creature continued. "You called him 'King,' for a time. Now look at him."

The stabbed youth began to rise again, only for the mummified corpse to once more re-plunge the dagger deep into his chest.

Rachel noticed Douglas take a step forward

out of the corner of her eye, his brain-box stumbling on its little legs as it struggled to keep up. "That's St. Edward the Martyr!" he gasped. "King of all England. Murdered in 979 during a struggle for the throne. His body is . . . *was* . . . buried here. What are you doing to him, you absolute shit?"

The mummified cadaver laughed again. "So he's a Saint as well as royalty? What am I doing to him? What did you do to him? Your King is as you made him. Weak. A symbol of failure. His role was that of a martyr. His one purpose in life was to die. He has no other function."

"Talking of death," said Rachel, "you're not looking too shabby yourself, for a reanimated corpse. And I can't help but notice you look better than the last time we met. You also seem to have gained the power of speech."

"Ah yes, I have found my tongue again, quite literally. Amongst other body parts. Look." The mummy yawned, its mouth opened wide and delicately poked out the shriveled meat of its tongue. Gripping the flesh with one gnarled hand, the creature tugged violently, until it came away with a sound like ripping Velcro.

The meat landed upon the altar cloth with a wet slap. No sooner had it landed than the gristly lump of flesh began to move of its own volition. Slug-like, the severed tongue inched its way across the altar towards its owner. The creature grinned as his tongue slowly crawled onto its lap, made its way up its chest and back into his open mouth. "And you are mistaken in referring to me as re-animated, woman." he said, thickly. "That is the same mistake my enemies made. They hacked the organs from my body, buried my parts in canopic jars, but the truth

51

is that no part of me has ever truly died. That is my gift. That is my curse. This sainted martyr before you lived only to die, a pleasure I can never take. But then he was never really a King, for how can there be succession when the rightful King still lives?

"I am the King. The Undying King. I am Caratacus, and my reign shall last for eternity."

There was a brief silence, before a lugubrious voice cut through the stillness of the church. "Oh, how bloody awful. Poor old you."

"What?"

Rachel looked on in wonder as Michael sauntered past her down the aisle, his hands deep in the pockets of his leather coat, floppy fringe hanging moodily over his eyes, as if unmindful of the fact that he walked amongst the living dead.

"No, I mean it. How utterly ghastly. You're what . . . thousands of years old, right? And you can never die? Dude, that's so sad. Because without death, life is meaningless, you know? I mean, to live forever is to suffer forever, right?" The Sulk stopped at the foot of the altar and flung his arms wide. "Big guy, I feel your pain, I really do. Your tale is just breaking my heart."

Caratacus leaned forwards, an expression of interest creasing his papyrus-like skin. Suddenly his hand shot towards Michael like a striking snake. Rachel heard a brief snapping sound, followed by a tiny whimper. As she took a hesitant step towards the altar, she realized that something was very wrong. Caratacus was holding something small and red in the palm of his hand, a glistening wet something that stretched on meaty strings back to a fist-sized hole in Michael's chest. The object rocked and trembled in the mummy's hand like a frightened bird. Caratacus held it up towards Michael's face, as though present-ing him with a trophy. "This organ causes you pain? I shall remove it, then. I am not without mercy."

Caratacus gave a violent tug of his arm, snapping the remaining arteries, before tossing The Sulk's heart contemptuously over his shoulder. The organ hit the floor like an overripe tomato. Like a meat puppet whose strings had been cut, Michael Chance—The Incredible Sulk—keeled over and died.

And then everything went mad.

Multi-Bird Roast With Spicy Pork Stuffing
(Serves Two)

"The funeral was nice though, wasn't it?" said Oliver. "I mean, there was a lot of wailing and misery, but then again he'd have loved all that, wouldn't he?"

"That's true enough," replied Rachel. "How's your meal?"

"Oh, to die for, darling."

"Please don't joke, Ollie. No one would die for turducken, anyway."

"I don't know, I've heard of stranger things. Apparently when The Sulk's death was announced, there was a spate of suicides amongst his fans. Just couldn't bear to go on without him."

"Oh, come on." Rachel sighed. "The Sulk's fans used to top themselves even when he was alive. Every time Michael released a new recording the figures went through the roof. Funeral homes used to have to hire more staff just to cope with the demand. And remember that time when he tried to go on tour? Half the front row had slit their wrists before the end of the first song. He'd never have been able to have a real career in music with his powers. It was us or nothing, I'm afraid."

"I know, I know. But he was my friend. I still miss him."

"I'm sorry, Ollie. But he's at peace now, anyway."

Oliver laughed dryly. "Hopefully. There's a certain irony to him being buried at Brookwood Cemetery."

"God, don't remind me. Bloody zombies. That fight was something else."

"Wasn't it just, though? By the way, what did you say this stuff was again?" Oliver prodded at the multi-layered slice of meat on his table, as though checking it for signs of life.

"It's called turducken, apparently. An entire chicken stuffed inside duck, which is itself stuffed inside a turkey."

"It's all a bit . . . extravagant, isn't it?"

Rachel laughed. "Oh, it's nothing compared to the nineteenth century version. Apparently it contained seventeen whole birds, all nested within each other. Now that's what I call extravagance!"

"Good grief! I can't see that leaving much room for pudding! Say, did you want any dessert, Rachel?"

"Well—not here thanks, Ollie. I'm trying to build up an appetite, after all."

"Oh, really? For what?"

Rachel leaned across and whispered conspiratorially in Oliver's ear. "Do you fancy coming back to my place and finding out? Because, to be honest, Ollie, all this talk about stuffing is making me horny."

* * *

The sound of wet meat hitting the church floor seemed to act as a signal of some kind. One second Rachel was staring incredulously at The Sulk's

55

freshly crumpled form, and the next, the mass of living dead were breaking over her like a putrescent tide.

The dead were all about her, pummeling, kicking, punching. Fingers clawed into hooks tried to gouge out her eyes. Stubby-toothed jaws clamped about her armor-plated limbs like the mouths of hungry infants. She felt her scalp begin to tear as rotting arms grabbed handfuls of her crimson hair and pulled.

Rachel thrashed madly in an attempt to throw her attackers off, but the sheer weight of numbers held her down. The bodies of the dead began to block out her vision, entombing her within the guts of a vast fleshy pyramid. The heady tang of overly-ripe flesh overwhelmed her senses, a sickening claustrophobia rising within her like a drowning black tide. Rachel opened her mouth to scream, only to feel questing fingers wriggle inside her mouth like fat, flaccid worms. She bit down hard, and the appendages broke off with a series of firecracker snaps, leaving her breathlessly gagging on the fleshy stubs.

And then, impossibly, the press of bodies began to ease. Rising from her enforced crouch, Rachel pushed the remaining zombies away from her with contemptuous ease. The dead suddenly seemed to be weightless, as if their bodies had been freed from the restraints of gravity. As the corpses fell away from her, they drifted into the mass of their already prone colleagues as though drawn by magnetism. Each corpse became a brick in a fleshy wall that now arced out around the front of the church.

"Telekinesis was never my strong point, but I can hold them back for a while." Brainbox stood motionless before the dead, his lips pressed tight in a grimace of pain. An arm's length away the corpses seemed to be pressed flat against nothingness. Like lifeless mimes, their hands clawed uselessly at the invisible barrier before them as they attempted to breach Douglas' psychic defence. "Leave the rank and file to me," Douglas grunted, his voice betraying the strain of his task. "Just stop Caratacus—he's the key!"

Rachel glanced across at Oliver, who nodded a silent affirmation, and China Doll and Mr. Oleaginous sprang into action.

Rachel reached Caratacus first, winding the Undying King with a hammer-like punch to the gut. Without pausing for breath, she continued to rain the blows down upon the animated mummy, who reeled under the assault. Rachel felt her body fat begin to cook beneath her armor as she drew upon her power reserves and knew that her time was limited. She had to finish this now. Blow by blow, she forced Caratacus down onto his knees. Attempting to flee, the mummy flipped over onto its back, but before it could scuttle off, Rachel stomped down hard, pinning the Undying King by the throat. "Not this time, mister!" she yelled, grinding her ceramic boot harder upon the monster's scrawny neck. "You're going nowhere!"

Rachel felt Oliver's presence alongside her, and a fine rain of back spray suddenly peppered her as Mr. Oleaginous blasted Caratacus full in the face with a jet of his oily sweat. The noxious body moisture poured out of Ollie's outstretched palms in twin streams, the fatty fluid bubbling and gurgling in Caratacus' open mouth as the monster tried to speak.

"That's it, Ollie!" roared Rachel. "Pour it on! Drown the son-of-a-bitch!"

For a full minute, Oliver kept the flood at full intensity, but eventually, inevitably, his reserves began to run dry. What was once a roaring river of sweat soon became a stream, which in turn, gave way to a feeble trickle. Oliver roared in frustration as he dredged the last drops of moisture up through his fingers, before rocking back on his heels, utterly spent.

Caratacus gurgled, turned his cadaverous head to one side and vomited a thin stream of clear liquid. His body began to shake, and a strange regular barking sound began to issue from his withered lips. It took Rachel a moment to realize he was laughing. "Fool! You cannot drown an immortal!"

Taking advantage of the moment of pause, Caratacus slipped his hands around Rachel's boot and twisted her off balance. Incensed, she pulled the struggling creature to its feet and struck back as hard as she could. Caratacus' head snapped back on his shoulders at the force of the initial blow, and she followed up with a sweeping kick to the creature's abdomen. The impact sent Caratacus sailing backwards through the air, until his form collided with the life-sized crucified Christ that stood sentry behind the altar. His mummified corpse a stain of rusty brown against the alabaster icon, Caratacus unpeeled himself like a scab from the skin of Jesus and dropped heavily to the floor.

Rachel took one step towards the walking corpse, but it turned and fled, limping past the choir stalls and out through a wooden side door. Sensing that victory was imminent, Rachel followed in the mummy's wake, bursting from the church into the light of day, only to be immediately brought short by the sight that awaited her.

The last time Rachel had seen the dinosaur was upon entering the Natural History Museum at the start of all this madness. Freed of its academic confines the Diplodocus skeleton looked even more imposing. From nose to tail, the creature stretched out to over a hundred foot in length, with the tip of its head looming over twenty feet above her. Sparks of blue fire raced about the monster's bones like blood pumping through invisible veins, as the creature pulsed and juddered with an impossible life. As she paused, stunned by the sight, Caratacus climbed up one of the monster's forelegs and crouched inside the open cocoon of its barrel-like ribs. Swinging gently from side to side, the mummy hung within the dinosaur's chest like a cancer-ridden heart, his body plainly visible through its blackened fleshless bones.

"What next, Caratacus?" called Rachel, her voice betraying the nerves she had hoped to hide. "Hiding in plain sight? This isn't going to help you."

"Fear not, woman. My mount shall yet have flesh on his bones. Knox—attend me!"

A ragged collection of corpses had begun to emerge from within the church, and Rachel noticed one of the shambling creatures take a step ahead of its fellows. The blue animating fire seemed to coagulate with a greater consistency about this portly cadaver, all but obscuring its expensive but ancient clothes. At the corpse's heels, two familiars trotted like excitable dogs, and Rachel recognized them as the two zombies from the train. Burke and Hare, the most infamous body-snatchers in history, ironically plucked rudely from the earth's embrace. In death, as in life, they followed in the wake of their one time employer.

The trio came to a halt at the foot of the dinosaur skeleton, and the zombified Doctor Knox threw his arms open wide. "These hands!" he cried suddenly in a high-pitch voice tinged with madness. "These hands are healing hands!" The blue fire blossomed within Knox's chest, welling from every pore. "Let sinew and muscle knit to bone! Let that which is incomplete be healed by the appliance of science! Give us the flesh, Lord, and we have the means! Yes, my friends—we have the technology!"

Blue flames erupted from Knox in a mass of jagged shards, shooting into the air before raining down upon the waiting horde of the living dead. The mass begun to shudder and shake as though in the grip of epileptic seizures, then, one after the other, the zombies began to walk towards the skeletal dinosaur.

"I'm sorry, Rachel. I just couldn't hold them any longer."

Rachel turned to see Douglas emerging from the church, his exhausted frame flattened up like windkill against the glass of his mechanically mobile brain-box. The construction supported his weight with ease as it gently shuffled forwards on its stubby metal legs, its overworked contents turning over gently behind him like beans coming to the boil. Trailing in the construct's wake lurched Mr. Oleaginous, his body similarly crumpled by exertion. "What are they doing now?" he asked, his dry voice matching his desiccated frame.

"I'm not entirely sure," Rachel replied, "but I think we ought to stop this sooner rather than later."

The shuffling brain-box halted at Rachel's side, and Douglas dropped to his knees, impacting upon the grassy turf with a solid thud. "I think we're already too late, Rachel—look!"

As they walked towards the skeletal dino-saur, Rachel could see that the zombies appeared to be losing stature, their bodies slowly miniaturizing as though a cameraman was matching their progress with a constant outward zoom. Step by step, the un-dead were regressing into youth, their broken bodies knitting together, their sallow wrinkled skin becom-ing ruddy and taut. Naked skulls grew egg-like bala-clavas of skin, which in turn sprouted ever thicken-ing clumps of hair. Within seconds, ranks of listless silvery manes blossomed into a multicolored crop of healthy blondes and browns and reds.

"Caratacus is controlling time!" Douglas breathed. "That's how he brought them back to life in the first place. He doesn't re-animate the dead, so much as regresses them backwards through time. But what's he doing now?"

Whatever process Caratacus was fueling, the outcome seemed to affect only the dead themselves, and not the suits and shrouds that variously clothed them. As they regressed from men and women to boys and girls, the unchanged garments appeared to devour their wearers. Heads shrank into collars, arms drew back into sleeves, until the very clothes them-selves appeared to be animate creatures, shuffling across the grass in some boneless fashion parade. As the age and height of the wearers steadily reduced, so finally the walking apparel would topple and fall, till from betwixt buttoned shirts and crumpled skirts would emerge the wriggling forms of naked babes. One undead child was momentarily trapped within a pair of cotton trousers, eventually emerging from one leg like a writhing snake before continuing upon its onward journey.

Having reached the foot of the dinosaur, the

infants began to climb, swarming grub-like over each other until they covered the bare bones of the long-extinct animal in a glistening wall of baby pink skin. Tiny hands clutched at each other, until grasping their neighbors the undead babes began to fashion their bodies into an interconnected hide of youthful flesh. As the process continued the rotten heart that animated the beast was slowly hidden from view, but before the human jigsaw completely occluded Caratacus, he issued one final instruction to his minions. "You too, my helpful familiars. Protect your King."

Seemingly against their own volition, Knox, Burke and Hare began to take hesitant steps forward, their bodies immediately beginning to shrink inside their suits. Burke and Hare began to shout at Doctor Knox, their voices harsh with terror. "Knox, you bastard! You set us up! You set us up!"

Soon, the trio were lost amongst the mass, and slowly the newly-fleshed dinosaur turned its baby-coated head towards what was left of Caratacus' enemies.

"Oh, shit."

And then it was upon them, the size of its monstrosity blocking out the midday sun. The creature raised one of its forelegs and Rachel threw herself to one side. With an earth-shaking thump, the baby-matted limb connected with the ground, the heavy impact throwing clods of dirt up into the sky. In the confusion of violence, Rachel heard a man's agonized cry, and glancing back, she saw Oliver's crumpled form pinned to the ground. His skin battered and bruised, Oliver writhed beneath the dinosaur's weight like a stuck bug, his inability to wriggle free a testament to his drained sweat reserves.

The creature moved again, and Rachel instinctively dodged the blow, but Brainbox wasn't so lucky. The creature had noticed Douglas attempting to run, the cumbersome box that carried his brains slowing him down, and with a contemptuous flick of its tail, the corpse-encrusted dinosaur swatted the psychic to the turf.

"Rachel . . . please . . . you have to stop it!" Douglas' arms flailed helplessly as he lay beside his toppled box, the weight of the container crushing his legs beneath its mass.

"I . . . I can't!" Rachel stuttered. "I can't hit them—they're just babies!"

The dinosaur turned its head in her direction and roared, its bellowing voice a choir of screams torn from a dozen infant throats.

"They're already dead, Rachel, and we will be too, if you don't do something soon!"

In truth was it wasn't just the corpse's infant forms that worried Rachel. Her body had reached its natural limit, and she simply didn't know how much longer she could last. Her teammates might not be able to see it, but she knew that within the concealing confines of her ceramic armor her once blubbery flesh had burned itself thin with the expenditure of energy. Her reserves nearly expended, Rachel felt less like a superhero and more like a bag of skin and bones. Much longer and she'd be indistinguishable from a zombie herself.

"Need a hand, Rachel?" The voice sounded like mud, and yet it seemed somehow oddly familiar. She felt a gentle touch upon her shoulder and glanced down. The hand that lay upon her was gloved in blue ethereal flames, and suddenly the identity of the man at her shoulder became clear. She knew who this was, but she couldn't face him. Not anymore. Not like this.

The Sulk's corpse began to sing a wordless keening dirge, the mournful notes encompassing all the misery of human existence, and Rachel hurriedly clapped her hands over her ears. The dinosaur stopped its approach and raised its long neck into the air, matching The Sulk's song with a plaintive cry of its own. Suddenly, the creature's borrowed flesh began to ripple. The animal's hide shook like a tree in a storm, and a rain of soft fleshy fruit began to fall. As infant corpses dropped from its bones, the blue fire at the dinosaur's heart began to bleed into view, Caratacus thrashing madly in its midst. "Idiot corpse! Your only will is my will! Obey your King or die once more!"

Rachel felt the hand gripping her shoulder tighten, and Michael's voice began to falter. She looked back down at his hand, only to see it become bone, then dust. His cadaver accelerated through time, The Sulk expired once more, but his sacrifice had given her the chance she needed.

Gathering her last reserves of strength, Rachel flung herself into the air and impacted with the dinosaur skeleton. Caratacus screamed in frustration as she began to snap the animal's rib cage apart, exposing his rancid hide to view. Rachel plucked the mummy from within the creature's chest and flung him to the floor. Deprived of its master, the Diplodocus skeleton followed suite, collapsing to the ground in a shower of bones.

Running on adrenaline, Rachel threw herself at the prone form of Caratacus, raining a succession of blows down upon him. Her gloves fractured with the force of the blows, the punches tearing her knuckles into bloody shreds. Rachel's body burned as though on fire, a billowing steam rising up through the neck of her armor as she burnt through calories at a prodigious rate. The fire fanned brightly for but a brief moment, and then she felt her blows becoming weaker. Rachel could feel her belly shrinking to nothing and beyond, her power beginning to draw upon the nutrients of her vital organs in a desperate attempt to maintain her energy levels. She felt a yawning sickness inside, the beating of her heart swelled into a hammering thud in her ears, and a terrible blackness began to edge in at the side of her vision.

Then it all went dark.

* * *

After an unknowable time, a flickering light seemed to lash against the darkness, and gradually, Rachel's vision began to return. The mummified form of Caratacus lay still beneath her, but both the corpse and the muddy ground beneath seemed washed out and devoid of color—a faded monochrome photograph, rather than reality itself. Her left hand gripped the Undying King tightly by the throat, while her right hand was raised above her head, ready to inflict another pummeling blow. Despite the violence of her actions however, her limb's motion had been curiously stilled, leaving her posed like a statue frozen in time. Gently, Rachel willed her hand to move downwards and was alarmed to see her body apparently divide into two. The still outline of her arm's original position remained firmly in place, while an echo of her adjusted limb projected through it in a ghostly overlap.

"Oh my God. Am I dead?"

"Not yet."

Rachel turned at the voice, her face breaking through the fragile outline of its own ethereal likeness as though it was a sugar glass shell. Drifting alongside her hung the pastel shade of Brainbox, a motion blur trailing behind his outstretched legs like some monstrous tail. Rachel followed the course of the tail backwards, finding it led to where Douglas' physical body lay trampled in the dirt several feet away. While his frozen physical form lay pinned beneath the weight of his toppled brain-box, Douglas' phantasmal echo bobbed weightlessly above, tethered to his remains like some ghostly balloon. Freed of its glassy confines, the elongated mass of his spectral brains floated gently alongside his head in an orbiting halo.

"Is this your doing, Brains?"

Douglas smiled. "Guilty as charged. I've taken advantage of Caratacus' distraction to slip us outside of reality and onto the psychic plane."

Rachel glanced down at the mummified form beneath her and shuddered. "So we're safe here, then?"

"Well, nothing can physically harm us here, but unfortunately we can't affect reality back. We're hidden in the gap between tick and tock, and being outside of the time stream, we are unable to affect anything we see. This is just a breathing space. We'll have to leave eventually. We can't stay here forever."

"I don't mean to seem ungrateful, Brains, but if that's the case, then why bring us here at all? Don't get me wrong, I appreciate the breather, but if it's just delaying the inevitable, then why bother?"

"Knowledge. I think it's become patently obvious that we're not going to defeat Caratacus in a test of brute strength. No offence, Rachel, but how are you going to defeat a man who cannot die? You can't keep hitting him forever. Eventually you will tire, and then what?"

Rachel paused before responding glumly. "I'll be honest with you, Brains, I don't think the real me has much fight left in her anyway. I'm practically burned out. Once we go back, I've got perhaps a minute—possibly less, before my strength gives out completely."

"Nevertheless, your actions today *have* provided us with a distraction. Caratacus is so busy fending you off that he's forgotten all about my psychic abilities."

"Couldn't you just—I dunno—fry his mind or something?"

"I've tried, believe me. But there's something blocking me, some barrier in this ancient mummy's head that I just can't break through. And there are still far too many questions. How did Caratacus become immortal anyway? How can he control time? What does he actually want? If we're going to defeat this Undying King, we have to find out what made him this way. We have to go into the past."

"You always told me there was no such thing as time travel."

"There isn't, as such. But Caratacus' memories are a frozen snapshot in time, and thanks to my powers, we can see whatever is rattling around in this walking cadaver's head. Fancy a peek?"

Douglas took Rachel by the hand, and together their spirits swooped towards the skull of the recumbent mummified corpse.

* * *

The man on the cart was naked and bound in chains. Discolored bruises and jagged scars pock-marked his flesh like a rash of stigmata. He gazed out defiantly at the assembled crowd, seemingly ignorant of their jeers and laughter. The cart was at the head of a procession of smiling Centurions, their armor gleaming in the midday sun. As they passed, members of the crowd were casting petals at the soldiers, while others busied themselves hurling rotten fruit at their captive. The disparity between victor and victim could not have been greater.

Rachel looked uneasily at the Centurions' sharp swords. "Are you sure they can't see us?"

"How can they? They're not real, just phantoms of the past. Caratacus' mind is a mess, but it seems that certain events have made a big enough impact to have lodged in his memory. We just have to hope that somewhere amongst them all is the key to unlocking the secret of his immortal power."

"Any idea what we're looking at now, Brains?"

"Well, according to the history books, Caratacus really was King of the Britons, but when he became a little too hungry for power, the Romans invaded, and this was his fate. Having defeated him, his victors brought him back to Rome, parading him through the streets as a trophy of war. Something for the citizens to gawk at, before they executed him. All this took place in the early years of the first century, just a short time after the death of Christ."

"So Caratacus should have died at this point in history?" Rachel moved closer to the cart, trying to match the face of the defiant captive with the withered countenance of the mummy two thousand years later.

"Well, no, not as such. Apparently, Caratacus managed to avoid execution with a nifty bit of public speaking. History records that before sentence was carried out he was given leave to address the Roman Senate, and somehow he managed to persuade them that he'd make a better example of Rome's greatness as a living subject than a dead martyr. And so, they freed him." The image of the procession began to flicker and change as Douglas spoke, almost as though he were physically flicking through the pages of a photo album. "It was always presumed that Caratacus had lived out the remainder of his life here in Rome, but evidently that was a little too close for comfort for Emperor Claudius. So, banned from his homeland, and barred from Rome, where might our mummified friend fetch up, do you think?"

"Well—Egypt presumably?"

"Precisely. Aegyptus, as it was then known at the time, was under Roman rule during the first century, and where better to send a troublesome one-time British King?"

The flickering images solidified, and Rachel and Douglas suddenly found themselves standing upon a golden plain. Moonlight cast eerie shadows across the landscape, transforming undulating dunes of sand into liquid waves upon a storm tossed sea. To one side, Rachel could make out the lights of a town, the sound of water lapping hungrily at a distant shoreline. Before them rose the seemingly endless expanse of the desert, its boundaries marked by a wall of immense pyramids that pointed defiantly up at the distant stars. Standing at their feet was the figure of a man, his arms aloft, his robes billowing fluidly in the nighttime breeze. The figure threw back his head and yelled at the sky.

"Well, there's Caratacus again," said Rachel, "but what's he up to now?"

"I'm not sure. Praying?"

Rachel took a step forward, trying to make out individual words in the one-time King's tortured cries. "But to who, exactly?"

Suddenly the ground beneath them began to shake, and Caratacus dropped to his knees. A tortured moan rent the heavens above, and a blazing hole of light ripped open like a tear in the sky. From within the hole an object appeared, a shining metal trapezoid that forced its way through the gap with a trumpeting squeal before falling towards the ground below. The object was wreathed in guttering blue flames, and Rachel swiftly recognized the unearthly energies that had earlier animated Caratacus' undead slaves. As the object descended, the fire pooled about its lower half, slowing the craft's progress until it descended smoothly upon a column of cerulean light. The blue blaze engulfed Caratacus as the object landed, momentarily hiding his swaddled form from sight, until a sudden gust of wind swept through the pyramids and parted the flames as though they were naught but a light mist.

As the view cleared, Rachel noticed a thin sheet of metal extending from one side of the craft, the gleaming substance angling downwards until its far end came to rest in the sand by Caratacus' prostate form. A hatchway sphinctered open in the side of the trapezoid, and something moved within.

"Jesus H. Christ!" Rachel gasped as a figure emerged and began to walk down the ramp. "Literally!"

Forgetting his phantasmal form, Douglas gulped nervously. "I . . . I think you may be right."

The figure looked human, a bearded man clothed in simple white robes, his face a mixture of infinite kindness and infinite sadness. A crown of thorns was jammed cruelly onto his head, thin rivers of red scoring his face where the thorns had pricked the skin. The man held out his open hands to the gibbering Caratacus, and Rachel noticed that long metal nails had been driven through each of the man's palms. Droplets of blood dripped from the ends of each nail, their spatter turning the golden sand red.

Rachel turned her ghostly outline towards Douglas. "I don't believe this, Brains. It's Jesus Christ. In a spaceship. Is there any way this thing could *possibly* get any more fucked up?"

"Oh, Lord!" cried Caratacus. "I seek your blessing! I seek vengeance upon my enemies! I seek the life everlasting!"

Jesus smiled kindly at the man before him. "My son. To know the life everlasting, all you need to do is open yourself, and let me in. Can you do that?"

"Yes, Lord! Yes! I give myself to you, willingly! Enter me! Please!"

Jesus gently cradled Caratacus' head in his hands. The nine-inch steel nails that were hammered through Christ's palms barely grazed the skin on either side of his temple.

Until he began to push.

* * *

The desert was alive with death.

A dull heartbeat seemed to pulse within the land itself, the ground echoing with the muffled thud of the buried dead as they hammered their way free

71

of enclosing stone-walled tombs. Having gained their freedom, the unbreathing mummies swum steadily upwards through the granular sea, their ban-daged-wrapped hands serving as ready-made scoops. One by one, they breached the surface of their sandy graves, their bodies sprouting like exotic flowers from the lifeless depths. Their corpses were limned with blue fire, the coruscating energy casting an eerie glow across the night-dimmed sand. Caratacus stood in the mummies midst, arcs of fire depending from his outstretched arms. He worked the undead like a puppeteer, raising them up upon ribbons of fire, be-fore casting them forth towards the distant lights of civilization.

Screams drifted across the night air as the first of the shuffling monstrosities entered the outskirts of the city. A blast of horns, a call to arms, and the de-fence began to form. Sounds of fighting rang out as Roman soldiers began to engage the initial invaders. The Centurions attacked the walking dead with a fe-rocious determination, gradually overwhelming their foes with sheer force of numbers. The tide of dead broke upon their ranks, and the soldiers emerged in masses from the city and began to march.

On the desert plain, the opposing forces met, a wave of mummified corpses encircling the regi-mented Roman army. The monsters attacked, and soldiers screamed as they were torn savagely in two, their warm guts spilling rudely onto the dusty sand. Swords stabbed and slashed in response, and the ground was soon littered with bandaged arms and heads, the severed appendages wriggling in the sand like agitated grubs.

Rachel and Douglas watched the scene from afar, their ghostly forms bobbling gently above the battle like tethered balloons.

"Well," said Rachel, "there goes another great misconception. For all these years people have been blaming grave robbers for breaking into the tombs of the dead. Who'd have guessed it was actually the mummies breaking their way out?"

"I think we can presume that this was Caratacus' attempt at revolution," said Douglas. "There's only one way this can end, of course."

"I just don't see how any of this can help us, though," replied Rachel. "The Romans are sustaining massive amounts of casualties. They're only winning by weight of numbers. Not exactly an option available to us back in the real world."

"Perhaps. But let's see what happens after the fight is over, shall we?"

* * *

The Romans slit Caratacus' throat, and he smiled. They stabbed him through the heart, and he barely noticed. They set his flesh ablaze, but though it blistered and boiled, his motions never truly ceased. One bright spark decided to remove the Briton's head, but it simply slithered across the floor on worm-like tendons before reattaching itself to his body. They tried to kill Caratacus in every way they knew how, and still he lived.

Finally, in desperation, they turned to the Egyptians.

Rachel tried to stifle a sense of nausea as the priests cut Caratacus open. She tried to tell herself that as she didn't currently possess a corporeal body, then she wouldn't be able to vomit anyway, so what was the point of feeling sick? It didn't help. Caratacus' guts spilled into his lap in a wet, red tide. His innards steamed gently with internal body heat, the foul stinking fug warring with the heady smell of incense in the enclosed temple vault. Instantly, the organs were alive with motion, juddering and shaking like salmon as they tried to swim back upstream and into the comforting embrace of Caratacus' ribcage. One by one, the priests captured the wriggling tubers of meat and separated them from their fellows with long curving blades. A number of clay jars were waiting on a dais nearby, their uncovered lids embossed with the profiles of various animal-headed gods. With the aid of tongs, the priests carefully transferred the squirming hunks of flesh to their new homes and sealed them fast.

Turning from the Canopic jars, the priests returned their attention to the subject at hand. Caratacus was chained to a stone altar, his now excoriated physique writhing in a desperate attempt to free itself. The priests had already removed his tongue, sick of the endless torrent of abuse and insults that had issued forth, but a wordless moan still issued from the Undying King's throat. The sound increased in intensity as one of the priests took up a large metal hook and inserted it roughly into Caratacus' nostrils. Rachel had to turn her shade away as the priest rammed the implement home. The sound of snapping cartilage and scraping meat sounded even over Caratacus' wordless screams, and Rachel turned to Douglas more for a distraction than anything else. "What are they up to now?"

"Removing the brain. They'll use that hook to mash it up, then drain it out through the nostrils."

"Oh, God!"

"Quite. Ironically, despite preserving all the

other organs, the ancient Egyptians considered the brain a completely useless lump of meat. So they just threw it away."

Rachel chanced a quick glance at Caratacus and saw a thick snail-trail of grayish meat spattering out of his nose. "Hold on though, I don't get it. You said we are currently sifting through Caratacus' memories, right? Well, how can we be, if his brain was destroyed all these years ago?"

"That's a very good question, Rachel. I can think of only two possible answers. Firstly, we've seen that Caratacus' powers of survival are off the scale. It's possible that even after this amount of damage his gray matter lived on, and body and brain were reunited at some point during the last two thousand years."

"And the other?"

"The other possibility is, frankly, somewhat more disturbing. Remember that thing in the desert?"

"Jesus, do you mean?"

"Well . . . something that Caratacus' addled mind *perceived* as Jesus, anyway. Do you remember what it did with those nails?"

"I can hardly forget."

"Well, look closer—you can just about make out the puncture wounds from here."

Rachel risked drifting closer, trying to ignore the violence being done to Caratacus, and focusing on the wounds on either side of his temple. The priests were beginning to envelop Caratacus' body with linen, and she suddenly realized that the mummification wrappings weren't there to preserve him, but to bind him.

"Well," continued Douglas, "let's suppose that that thing in the desert put itself, or a part of itself, inside Caratacus' head. Somehow it transmitted itself down those nails and inside. It would account for Caratacus' new found power, after all. Now, let's presume that the force then spreads throughout his body, gifting Caratacus with immortality in the process. Well, perhaps it's still there two thousand years later, the same parasitic entity, clinging grimly onto the echo of Caratacus' thoughts. I expect it's completely insane after two thousand years of captivity. It probably doesn't even realize that it isn't Caratacus anymore."

"But if Caratacus' brain is gone, then that would mean that we're . . . "

"Traipsing through the memories of the creature that possessed him, yes. A creature that fell through a tear in the fabric of the universe and latched on to this poor old King's thoughts. Rachel, I do believe we're dealing with an alien entity here."

"Oh Lord. This just gets better and better. So we're currently drifting through an alien's mind. Do you think it knows we're here?" Rachel stooped over and peered at the smooth hole that impacted the right-hand side of Caratacus' temple. It took her a moment to realize that another eye was staring back at her from within the hole. "Shit—it's seen me. I think it's waking up!"

The scene began to flicker and shudder like a badly tuned television. Rachel fled back towards Douglas' shade, but he seemed to be drifting in and out of reality as well. "Rachel! We haven't much time, Caratacus—the creature—it's pulling us out of the psychic plane!"

"But what can we do?" she asked, panic stricken. "If the priests couldn't get that entity out of Caratacus' body, how the hell will we be able to?"

"We may not able to, Rachel—but I do have something in mind. A joker in the pack, if you will. Rachel, when we get back, I need you to do something for me. Forget Caratacus for the moment—we can't beat him with brute strength. I need you to release my brains."

"What?"

"It's time for me to think outside of the box."

* * *

After the dreamy languor of the psychic plane, the transition back to reality was too sudden, too intense. One moment Rachel was drifting as weightless as a cloud, the next she was slammed back into her body. The sensation was like being hit by a car. The color, the noise, the texture of Caratacus' body beneath her—reality itself seemed *too* real, like a television whose contrast and color had been turned up to the max. Rachel reeled under the onslaught, and immediately the mummy beneath her was free.

Caratacus swatted Rachel aside as if she was a fly, the rake of his claw-like hands leaving a series of jagged marks scored across her face. She pitched forward into the churned-up ground, her spineless swoop sending clods of mud up into the air.

Exhausted, Rachel lay motionless on the ground, her head turned to one side, the smell of dirt and defeat clogging her nostrils. This was it. She couldn't do any more. The fight had robbed her of every last ounce of energy. She had nothing left. She could only imagine how badly the overuse of her powers had drained her once flabby physique. A sudden memory of a nursery song her mother used to sing to her suddenly stole into her mind, some line about a too-small baby being washed down the plughole. How did it go, again? Ah, yes, "*Just like a skeleton, wrapped up in skin.*" On some level, Rachel knew her mind was wandering, knew that her energy starved brain was shutting down. She just didn't care anymore.

And then she heard Douglas calling her. "Rachel! Wake up! Help! Please!"

Feeling as though a ten-ton weight was balanced on her neck, Rachel wearily pulled her head upright and gazed across the battlefield.

Douglas was struggling with the brain-box that lay atop him, writhing beneath its weight. The psychic warrior slapped his hands ineffectually at its sides, as though trying to wake his sleeping brains. Rachel could see that one side of the box had become cracked in the fight, and a thin stream of fluid oozed from the glass wound like jam leaking from a doughnut. Gritting her teeth at the pain, she began to crawl towards him.

The churned-up grass between them was littered with debris. Regressed zombie infants crawled sluggishly between broken shards of dinosaur bones, and Rachel flicked them out of her way as she progressed. Beneath one larger mass of collapsed bones Rachel could make out Oliver's supine form. His body appeared to have been partially crushed, but the rapid rise and fall of his chest told her that Mr. Oleaginous still lived. Good. Let someone come out of this mess alive.

Rachel was within five feet of Douglas' body when she felt a hand close around her ankle. She looked behind her and saw a hideous leering rictus grin. Caratacus! Pinning her to the ground, the monster reached out one paw and pulled free the ceramic plate that encased her lower left leg. He smiled at her, almost lovingly, then leaned forward and bit a chunk of flesh out of her calf. The pain was a searing heat of agony, but from somewhere it lent her a fresh leash of desperate energy, and she pulled her limb free. Propelling herself through the mud like a seal, Rachel covered the last few feet to fetch up panting alongside her fallen colleague.

"The box!" he cried. "Rachel—open the box!"

She saw that the hinged lid of the container was beyond Douglas' reach. Fearfully aware of Caratacus' nearness, Rachel dragged herself to her knees and reached upwards. Her hands found the catch, and she flicked it open, but the lid refused to rise. With a sense of grim fatality, she noticed that when the container had fallen its metal lid had been buckled out of true, and now it was wedged firmly shut. A smell of rotting meat was upon her, and Caratacus laughed in her ear. With a final scream of desperation, Rachel struck at the glass container with one armored fist. The cracked surface shattered, and her legs were suddenly covered in a syrupy red tide. She caught a momentary flash of gray-pink meat slopping to the floor, then fell backwards as Caratacus pushed her aside.

The Undying King stood over Douglas' broken brain-box like a hunter astride its fallen prey. His poached egg eyes swivelled wildly in their sockets, and he gazed appreciatively at the brains that had begun to spill out of the box. His rictus grin widened. "What's this? More meat for me? Ah—a feast fit for a King!"

Caratacus reached down into the mass of

quivering flesh and lifted something clear. The lobe was grossly distorted, a quivering mass of pinkish gray matter that looped and coiled about his arms like a skinned python. Caratacus pulled harder at the meat, the movement tugging on the stem that led through the roof of Douglas' open skull, causing the man to buck and writhe in the mud like a broken toy.

Caratacus glanced over to where Rachel was lying and smiled. "But where are my manners? I shouldn't talk with my mouth full." The mummy reached one hand up to his face and spat a lump of half-chewed gristle into his open palm. He tossed the meat towards Rachel, and she felt her stomach churn as she realized what it was. "You taste good, woman. I'll finish you later." Caratacus licked his lips and lifted the loop of Douglas' brains towards his mouth.

"Caratacus, please!" she begged. "Don't do this! If there's anything left of the real you—resist! That voice in your head—whatever it is—it's not Jesus! Don't listen to it! Let him go!"

The mummy pulled his head back and laughed, an asthmatic wheeze that rang out across the battleground like a steam train laboring uphill.

"It's alright, Rachel," groaned Douglas weakly. "I think our mummified friend here will soon find out he's bitten off more than he can chew. I told you I had something in mind, and I meant it literally."

"Eh? What trickery is this?" Caratacus released the loop of Douglas' brain and took a step back. The segment of meat fell back, reconnecting with its remaining mass with a wet slap. About half of Douglas' mutated gray matter now lay steaming gently on the grass, while the remainder had fetched up against one side of the toppled container. Rachel looked closer and gasped. The brains in the overturned box appeared to be moving of their own volition. The slobbery mess stirred sluggishly, as if awaking from sleep, then began to rise. The bloody mass expanded above its broken container like a baking cake, rising to a height of a foot clear of the box, before stilling.

In the awed silence that followed, Rachel became aware of a hissing gasp emanating from the meat, almost as though Douglas' brains were breathing. Gingerly, Caratacus reached out one hand and prodded the mass. A coil of the meat slid to one side, and it took Rachel a second to realize what she was looking at.

A blood-soaked face.

The blood-soaked, smiling face of a child.

A child small enough to have remained hidden within a glass case, nestled up amongst the fronds of Douglas' oversized brain matter as though it was the snuggest of duvets. One swollen lobe still lay atop the child's head like some blubbery beret, and she gently pushed it to one side. The girl's crown was encircled by blood-soaked bandages, one eye was swollen shut with livid purple bruises, and her left arm was encased in plaster—all trophies of her previous encounter with the mummy. Yet despite her battered appearance, Rachel had little difficulty in recognizing her injured colleague.

Little Miss Pester removed the oxygen mask that had sustained her during her hours of confinement. "Remember me, asshole?"

Caratacus moved to strike the child, but Lucy was quicker.

"You in the mummy—*show yourself!*"

Show YourSelfShow YourSelfShow YourSelf—the words echoed in Rachel's head, repeated an im-

81

possible number of times at an impossible speed, their hypnotic effect making her reel—but Caratacus was their unlucky target. The mummy clutched its hands to its head in agony as in staggered under the assault of Lucy's pester power. Caratacus wilted like a flower under the pressure, sinking first to his knees before keeling over face first to the ground. Despite its prone position, the creature's body continued to move, as though something inside it was thrashing about in desperation.

As Lucy's hypnotic chant continued, Rachel noticed thousands of pinpricks of light begin to appear upon the thrashing cadaver's body. The alien energy welled up through Caratacus' mummified pores like liquid spots of blue blood. The parasite howled, it screamed, it begged, but it was powerless to resist. Inch by inch, tendrils of blue fire were being drawn out, before coagulating together into a spumescent froth that hung weightless in the air above Caratacus' body like ghostly candyfloss. Finally, the parasite was free.

Lucy and the alien faced each other like a pair of macabre Russian Dolls, each having emerged from the shell of another. Having shucked off Caratacus' shell, the alien entity was now a shapeless mass of blue fire, hanging suspended in the air. Lucy's chant—*Show Yourself Show Yourself*—continued without respite, and the blue shape bucked violently. Suddenly, hanging upon the air in its place was an image of Jesus, his mouth open in a silent scream. Before Rachel had time to react, the image changed into a vision of a beautiful young woman, then changed again into an ancient, withered man. The alien flickered and strobed, spinning through an impossible kaleidoscope of human and animal forms as it desperately struggled against Lucy's command. Finally, the motion ceased and, all its masks exhausted, the creature stood revealed before them in all its terrible glory.

The alien parasite hung upon the breeze like some monstrous barrage balloon, its enormous size practically blotting out the sun. The creature as a whole was enmeshed in the familiar cerulean glow, the alien energy pulsing in steady contrails down its flanks as though it were some vast, pulsating squid. Its swollen blimp of a body seemed to be impaled upon a cluster of massive angular constructs, with organic curves and straight-edged lines coexisting in a furious melange. The opposing geodesic and geometric forms didn't so much abut each other as coexist in some disharmonious overlap. The effect was like trying to observe two different objects occupying the same place at the same time, and Rachel's eyes immediately stung with the impossibility of the task.

Studding the creature's carapace, like glittering jewels, were objects that might have been used for its own vision, the spherical orbs slatted and latticed like an insect's compound eyes. Closer towards the creature's core, Rachel noticed a constant furious motion, as skittering somethings raced about its hide like chitinous ants. Were these creatures an integral part of the parasite's own biological form, or merely an infestation of its own? The ant-like things paused intermittently on their interminable circumnavigation of the bloated entity, tugging and pulling at a succession of obscure organic nodules and lugs along the way. Perhaps these were the true aliens, she thought, piloting their insane biological craft through vast unknowable oceans of reality?

Rachel was so overwhelmed by the sight of the alien that at first she was unaware of its forward motion. Like a stealthy cat, the creature was edging ever nearer to Lucy's miniscule form. The girl seemed ignorant of its approach, her pestered command having tailed off into awed silence. Lucy had followed Douglas' mental instructions, but having revealed the alien's true form, she seemed unsure of what to do next. Vast unseen engines growled within the alien's depths, and Rachel noticed a huge distorted limb beginning to unfurl from within. The elongated appendage ended in a cruelly hooked barb, and Rachel thought back to the nail-wielding figure that had first infected Caratacus all those centuries ago. "Lucy, look out!"

It was too late—the girl was oblivious. Rachel desperately tried to drag herself to her feet. She had to stop this happening again, she had to stop the creature from infecting Lucy. But she simply had no energy left. Rachel's legs buckled and she collapsed back down into the mud. She howled in frustration. After all this! Please God, it couldn't end like this!

The voice she heard next was less of a triumphant rallying cry and more a dry croak. "Have no fear—Mr. Oleaginous is here!"

The barbed limb struck out like a snake, and suddenly Lucy was gone, her small frame having been pushed violently to one side. Oliver Rangarajan screamed as the spike punctured his temple and collapsed to his knees. Like a dose of bad medicine, the creature began to inject itself down the funnel of its own appendage, its enormous mass compacting impossibly as it syringed itself into Oliver's head. Within a few seconds, it was gone.

Rachel closed her eyes, her head face down

in the dirt, and waited for what would happen next.

* * *

She wanted to rest, wanted to sleep, but someone was clapping.

Rachel opened her mud-encrusted eyes and looked about at a scene of utter devastation. The grassy area beside the church was strewn with tiny doll-like corpses and blackened dinosaur bones. As she watched, the zombified infants slowly melted into the ground like aspirin dissolving in water. Caratacus followed swiftly behind, his mouth seeming to yawn wider in a smile of gratitude as his flesh dropped swiftly away from his ancient bones. The Undying King was finally at peace, and someone was clapping.

Douglas was back to his feet, and Lucy was gingerly helping him return his spilled brains back inside their toppled case. Beside the pair, Oliver's body lay still in the mud, a small circular hole clearly visible in his temple. He appeared to be asleep. And somebody was still clapping.

Rachel looked back towards the church and saw a man approaching, his palms connecting repeatedly in a series of enthusiastically meaty slaps. He was dressed in the stereotypical suit and bowler hat of a London banker, though his eyes were hidden behind chunky mirrored sunglasses. He was smiling, broadly.

The man began to walk towards Oliver's body, and she tried to call out a warning to hear teammates, but unconsciousness claimed her first.

FOURTH COURSE:
Just Desserts: A Little Light Supper
(Serves One)

Oliver paid off the taxi driver and followed
Rachel up the steps of the building opposite. The
apartment block was one of a row of converted
townhouses, their identical gleaming white exteriors
presenting an impressive but somehow anonymous
facade. He leaned against the black painted iron rail-
ings that segregated the house from the pavement
and chuckled as Rachel struggled with the front door.

"So, this is it. China Doll's secret hideaway.
What do you call it, then, 'The Doll House'?"

"Don't get too excited," Rachel replied, ushering him off of the street and into a narrow hallway.
"It's just a regular block of flats, and I'm not the only
tenant. Top floor."

Oliver led the way up the steeply angled staircase, ignorant of the thin snail-trail of moisture his
hand was leaving upon the wooden banister. "Mind
you. On what they pay us, I'm amazed you can af-
ford such a nice area."

Rachel laughed drily. "We're public servants,
Ollie. We do it for love, not money. Or hadn't you
heard?"

Oliver gained the top of the stairs and paused
outside an anonymous wooden door. He turned to
face Rachel, his eyes blotchy and unfocused. "Lord.
I do feel a little the worse for wear. I think I may have

eaten too much tonight."

Rachel smiled. "Come on, Ollie. You'd better get used to good living. No expenses spared in America, right?"

Oliver sighed heavily. "Look, Rachel—I'd be a fool to pass up this opportunity. I don't want to leave, but . . . America. They do things different there. You should come too. Have a word with Calvin, see what he can do."

"You're the one with the fancy new powers now, Ollie. And what would they want with me, exactly? Super strength? Jesus. There must be thousands of spandex-clad idiots running around America with my powers already." Rachel paused as she unlocked the door to her flat. "Besides which, I don't trust Calvin. Anyone who wears sunglasses indoors is a little too shifty for my liking."

Oliver followed Rachel inside, trying not to trip over the mass of discarded food packages and dirty plates that littered the floor.

"Sorry about the mess, Ollie. One of the curses of my power. My flatmate and I have learned to put up with it."

"Flatmate?"

"Yeah, he should be around here somewhere." Rachel saw Oliver's nonplussed expression and laughed. "Oh, Ollie, don't worry. You don't have any competition. Here comes Buggalugs now."

Oliver breathed a sigh of relief as the fat cat sidled into the room from an adjacent door, his tail angled in a furry question mark.

"Well, at least he's gentleman enough to leave the bedroom." Rachel took Oliver by one sweat-slicked elbow. "Come with me, superhero."

Oliver allowed himself to be led, but Rachel

could tell by the increasing flow of sweat that he was still nervous. She eased the bedroom door fully open and led him towards the single bed within. A gentle push upon his shoulders, and Mr. Oleaginous sat down heavily upon her duvet. With deliberate slowness, Rachel began to undo the buttons on his shirt, his nut-brown skin emerging inch by inch in a hesitant striptease. His abdomen was slicked with sweat, a running stream of moisture that began to spill over his lap and soak into the bed sheets. "Jesus, Ollie—I guess you never have to worry about lubrication."

Oliver dutifully laughed at the joke, but his heart wasn't in it. "Sorry, Rach. All this is a bit sudden. Are you sure you want to do this? Now? I'm just not sure I feel all that well."

"Oh, that's just your nerves, Ollie," Rachel smiled. "Well, either that or the poison I paid the chef to lace your food with. It should be kicking in just about now."

Oliver expelled a short barking laugh. "Yeah right, Rachel. What were you planning to do—date-rape me or something?" He smiled, but it froze on his lips when she didn't respond. "Rachel?" Oliver tried to stand, but his legs suddenly seemed incapable of supporting his weight and he flopped bonelessly back down upon the bed. His limbs felt numb, as though they had been buried in snow. At the edge of his vision he could sense Rachel moving, and dimly he felt her touch as she lifted his unresisting legs back onto the bed, laying him out flat. As the paralysis took hold, he felt uncomfortably like a corpse laid out for a family viewing. His lips felt like rubber, as though he'd had an injection to remove a tooth, and when he opened his mouth, the words came out muffled and indistinct. "Wha . . . ? Whut's gonn on?"

"Easy, Ollie, easy." Rachel moved outside of his vision for a moment. When she returned, she was carrying a large kitchen knife. "I'll try and make this quick."

Oliver seemed to be having some trouble moving his jaw. "Whu . . . what are you . . . going to do?"

She smiled, as though the answer was obvious. "Why, cut your throat, to begin with."

"Wha . . . are you . . . talkin . . . bou? Why?"

"You want to know why?" Rachel sighed, then began to undo her dress. "Poor Ollie. I think it would be easier to show you. You deserve that much, I suppose. After all, it's not like you're going to be telling anyone else what you've seen here tonight."

Rachel slipped her high-collared dress onto the floor, revealing a swathe of cotton cloth that covered her body from ankles to neck. The broad strips of material were looped about her figure like so many bandages, and Oliver was instantly reminded of Caratacus. Rachel clutched her hands to the generous contours of her covered breasts. "These? Don't get too excited, Ollie. Things are never quite how they seem." She tapped firmly at one breast, the sound betraying rigid plastic rather than yielding flesh. Laughing, she unhooked a safety pin that held the end of one bandage to its fellows and, essaying a gentle pirouette, began to unwrap herself. The unspooled wrappings gathered about her feet as she turned, until finally she stood naked before him in all her glory.

Oliver felt sick.

Beneath the carefully concealing artifice of her clothes, beneath the molded bodice that had duplicitously replicated her hourglass figure, Rachel

McFarland's body was repugnant. The curves of her once-womanly physique were lost amongst rubbery flaps of hollow skin, the hanging meat the result of years of rapid weight gain and energy expenditure. Its elasticity lost, Rachel's baggy skin was draped about her torso like an ill-fitting cardigan, making her look like a child caught attempting to wear their parent's clothes. The flesh about her legs wrinkled up like a pair of oversized bed socks, while the twin lumps of gristle that hung down around her waist could only be the withered remains of breasts. Worst of all was the stomach itself, the powerhouse of Rachel's daily bloat and purge, which hung slackly about her knees like an untanned leather skirt.

Displaying herself like some rare and fabulous bird, Rachel spread her arms wide. Oliver could see veins pulsing through the translucent skin that depended slackly beneath her limbs like pterodactyl wings. "You've got something I want Oliver. Something I need. So I'm going to take it. It's nothing personal; I just can't live like this anymore. You do understand, don't you?"

Oliver tried to speak, but the words just seemed to merge into one long inarticulate gurgle. Rachel cocked her head quizzically to one side and waited while he tried again. Oliver forced the words out one at a time, desperately trying to make his enunciation clear. "Wait! Can't . . . kill . . . me . . . now! I'm . . . immortal! Remember?"

Rachel picked up the kitchen knife and smiled. "Remember? In fact, I'm counting on it!"

* * *

The waiter seemed surprised to see her back

90

again so soon. "Madam has another appointment this evening?"

"Yes. It's all arranged with your boss. Mr. Merryweather?"

"Ah, yes, of course—the American gentleman. Right this way."

The waiter led her back towards the main area of the restaurant, back to the same table where she and Ollie had dined earlier that day. In Oliver's place was a small man wearing a business suit, bowler hat and sunglasses. He looked up from the menu at their approach. "Ah! Rachel—glad you could make it!"

"Calvin Merryweather. How do you do?" Rachel held out a hand to the man, who leaned forwards and pressed his lips to it.

"Charmed, Miss McFarland. Charmed. Please, won't you sit down?"

"I'd be delighted to. And may I once again apologize for Oliver's absence. As soon as the team can locate him, we'll let you know."

"Yes, I received your message earlier. Very strange, that Mr. Rangarajan should just vanish like that."

"Indeed."

"And at a time like this."

"Yes, it does seem odd, doesn't it?"

Calvin studied Rachel for a while, as though considering something. "I was looking forward to getting Mr. Oleaginous on board as soon as possible. The network is due to unveil the new line-up on Sunday, and an immortal would have been perfect for us. The shareholders will be so disappointed."

Rachel smiled. "Never mind. Who knows? Maybe you'll be lucky? Maybe another immortal superhero will turn up from somewhere?"

"Really? You think there might be more of those aliens out there? Is that what you mean?" Calvin furrowed his brow in thought. "Say—do you think that alien parasite thing might have sent Mr. Rangarajan a bit—I don't know—loopy? We're not going to have another Caratacus situation here are we?"

"Oh, I don't think so. Our alien friend was severely weakened by the fight, and Brains has been working hard on setting up a mental block to stop it from taking over Ollie's mind. It should be quite harmless now. Besides, for all we know Caratacus wasn't that stable to begin with. Did you know that when the alien crash-landed he actually thought it was Jesus?"

"Really? Pity I couldn't have been there to see that, it would have made for some interesting footage. Maybe we could do a mock up later? Then again, a lot of our audience are believers, and it's probably not a good idea to offend them in any way."

Calvin broke off as the waiter arrived bearing their meal. Silver dish covers were removed, and the table was wreathed in the smoke and smell of roast meat. Calvin leaned over the dish and breathed the steam in, savoring the aroma. When he looked up, Rachel was laughing.

"Calvin, your sunglasses are steaming up. Don't you think you had better take them off now?"

"Well, I suppose I have got all the footage I need now." Calvin reached up and removed the glasses, revealing pinched eyes that blinked in the gloom of the restaurant like a mole greeting the dawn. As he gently laid them on the table, Rachel got a glimpse of the complex recording circuitry embedded within.

"Can I have a look?"

"Be my guest."

Rachel put the glasses on. Within the inner display screen was frozen an image of herself seated at the restaurant table, as seen from Calvin's perspective.

"Here." Calvin reached out one hand and touched a hidden stud embedded in the edge of one of the earpieces. The image displayed on the inner lenses of the glasses began to change, flickering backwards in time as the video recording reversed. "There's the battle at the Church. Pity about The Sulk, of course. And that's the footage from the Natural History Museum. See? There's the bit where you first noticed me. I'll have to edit that out, or it will ruin the verisimilitude of the piece. It's crucial in documentary television to always maintain the illusion of reality. The cameraman has to be an observer, not a participant. It's my job to be invisible. I am nothing. I am no one."

"The ethics of being a talent-spotter, eh?"

"Exactly."

Rachel picked up her steak in both hands and tore a bloody chunk away. "I have to admit, though, that there is still one little thing which puzzles me about all of this."

"Oh yeah?"

"The alien. As far as our boffins can tell, its power revolves around manipulating time. It didn't so much re-animate those corpses as regress them through time to the point where they died, then used their shells as a ready-made army."

"Your point being?"

"Well, the problem with all that is the dinosaur bones. Because they aren't. Bones, I mean. That Diplodocus from the Natural History Museum is only a replica—a metal cast of a real dinosaur skeleton located in Pittsburgh. So the alien's power wouldn't have been able to affect it, and Caratacus shouldn't have been able to ride off on that hundred-foot long monstrosity." She smiled. "But then you wouldn't have got such impressive footage for the viewing public. Would you?"

Calvin looked shocked, or at least attempted to. "What—exactly—are you suggesting, Miss Mc-Farland?"

"Me? Nothing. Nothing at all. I just think it's interesting, that's all. So tell me, Mr. Merryweather, what's *your* power?"

The talent-spotter said nothing. He just smiled.

* * *

Once the paperwork was signed and it was all official, Rachel returned to her flat. The place was still a mess, she hadn't had time to clear up most of the blood before leaving for dinner with Calvin. Poor Oliver, he would have loved to have gone to the States. But then again, she supposed, he would. In a manner of speaking.

Rachel examined herself in the full-length bedroom mirror. After her double meal she was starting fill out a little, though she was still going to have to be careful about what outfit she chose for the official announcement. Something long and billowy. Something disguising. But it wouldn't have to be for long. Calvin had assured her that getting the plastic surgery was no problem—most of the network heroes had it these days, apparently. And once that excess skin had been removed, why—she could wear outfits as revealing as she liked. Her days of bloat and purge were over.

A mournful wail interrupted her train of thoughts, and Rachel turned to face her only real friend.

"Oh, Buggalugs, are you hungry again? I don't know where you put it all, I really don't." She moved towards his cupboard stash of tinned cat meat, before pausing. Eternity was a long time, and what would be the point of living forever if your best friend wasn't around to share it with you?

Her decision made, Rachel changed direction and headed towards the kitchen. She paused at the refrigerator, listening to the gentle sounds of tapping from within. It was getting restless, already. She'd have to work out some sort of secure storage for the trip to America. A small safe ought to do it.

Rachel opened the fridge. She had removed the dividing shelves earlier, and stuffed inside the resulting space was a gray Hessian sack, tied up with string. The sack was quivering, gently. Rachel untied the sack, reached in with a pair of long metal tongs and gently removed a small cube of bloody meat. As soon as the diced flesh hit the carpet it began to wriggle like a slug, but Buggalugs was faster. The greedy cat gobbled the bloody treat down, then turned to look at Rachel, licking his lips in anticipation of more.

"Good boy," she said. "Now, just make sure you keep it all down, and you'll never have to be hungry again."

She smiled. No more hunger. A single meal that would last forever. An infinite source of energy. The meat never dying, forever digesting, forever regenerating. No more binge eating. No more weight fluctuation. No more hiding. She could do anything, be anything, and always look like a million dollars.

Sometimes, she thought, just sometimes, good things happened to good people.

A sudden belch unexpectedly forced its way through her lips, echoing like a gunshot off the tiled kitchen walls. "Quiet down there, Ollie! Remember—I did tell you a body like mine takes sacrifice."

Rachel McFarland smiled at her own good fortune, savoring the sweet taste of success. Unnoticed, a thin tear of oil gently trickled from one side of her mouth.

About the Author

Lawrence Conquest lives in Bristol, England. His previous stories for Blood Bound Books are: The Face in the Sand (published in *Night Terrors*, honorable mention Best Horror of the Year 2010), Beneath the Trees (*Seasons in the Abyss*) Life to the Lifeless (*Steamy Screams*), and The Balancing Act (*Night Terrors II*). More info can be found at:
www.lawrence-conquest.blogspot.com